Fatal Destiny

*Purchased at the request of a
Libraries of Stevens County reader*

**Your recommendations and
Suggestions are welcome
www.thelosc.org**

Fatal Destiny

Frank J. Miller

Copyright © 2014 by Frank J. Miller.

Library of Congress Control Number:		2014908479
ISBN:	Hardcover	978-1-4990-1563-8
	Softcover	978-1-4990-1564-5
	eBook	978-1-4990-1560-7

All rights reserved. No part of this book may be reproduced or transmitted in any form or by any means, electronic or mechanical, including photocopying, recording, or by any information storage and retrieval system, without permission in writing from the copyright owner.

This is a work of fiction. Names, characters, places and incidents either are the product of the author's imagination or are used fictitiously, and any resemblance to any actual persons, living or dead, events, or locales is entirely coincidental.

Any people depicted in stock imagery provided by Thinkstock are models, and such images are being used for illustrative purposes only. Certain stock imagery © Thinkstock.

This book was printed in the United States of America.

Rev. date: 05/08/2014

To order additional copies of this book, contact:
Xlibris LLC
1-888-795-4274
www.Xlibris.com
Orders@Xlibris.com

CHAPTER I

The great diva sat in her dressing room. She looked into the mirror and adjusted her blond wig. *Well*, she thought, noticing the damage done to her face by the inexorable passage of time, *the years have certainly passed*.

"Madame, Madame," an incessant voice called, "you must be ready for act IV in a few minutes."

She answered in her almost baritonal voice. "Yes, darling, I'm coming." The white robes worn for the last act of *Otello* were meticulously draped around her. She hummed high into her head voice and mused. *Yes, it will all be in pianissimo. After all, that is what I am famous for. Oh, to face that damned Hungarian conductor again. I hate him and also am slightly afraid of him*. Then she laughed and began to think of the past. *The halcyon days under Toscani and Walter were the greatest, and so was I*. Alas, she said, "I still am."

These young singers! So much publicity! They come and go. One day, they are mezzos, the next day, sopranos. Always cancelling until they can sing nothing.

"Madame, Madame, you must be on stage at once!" She hurried to the wings and was soon singing "Salce, Salce." The high soft tones by some magic still filled the house. There was some difficulty as she knelt down before the Virgin to sing "Ave Maria." A few pounds and age had left the diva somewhat less mobile. However, she lifted the last notes of *ave, ave* high up into the back of her throat as she had done for over thirty years. Then Otello came on with murderous rage on his face. *I'll fight for my life*, she thought.

I'm not the whimpering type. After all, with me in this role, Desdemona becomes the leading part. She milked the scene for all it was worth. The curtain eventually fell, and she went before the crowd. The fans went wild. Desdemona was indeed the star of this evening. The fans threw flowers at her, and she put her hands to her mouth to give them kisses of appreciation. Even the conductor took her hand and went out for a bow with her. Madame did not care for this. *He's cashing in on my fans,* she thought, but went through the charade anyway. The general manager came to her dressing room afterward and asked her if she could be in his office on Tuesday morning the following week at 11:00 am. *Oh,* she thought, *he still wants me for another season. That season will be the last for this house.*

The next morning, she woke early and asked the maid, Anita, to bring hot chocolate and the morning newspaper to her bedside. Madame immediately turned to the entertainment area. There it was, the review of *Otello*. Not caring one iota what they said of the conductor or tenor, she only wanted to read about herself. vocal miracle at opera, the review read. "Diva over sixty sang beautifully. The audience didn't realize a vocal miracle had taken place." Madame didn't like her age being focused upon, nor did she like the words *vocal miracle.*

I was born with a great dramatic voice, she thought. Although lessons with Ternina, the great Wagnerian, had helped her, she recalled.

The phone rang, but she did not pick it up. Anita entered once more and asked if she would talk to Madame Regime, the highly respected French singer. *Oh, that bitch!* were the words that crossed her mind. "Yes, I will speak with her," she told Anita.

"Good morning, darling." Again in her sepulchral speaking voice.

"Bonjour, Madame. I'm always amazed to hear you speak in such low tones and then sing up to a high C with ease."

"Darling," she said, "high Cs, as you know, do not grow on trees, especially these days."

The conversation continued. Madame Regime went on, "I thought that maybe, just maybe, you could coach me in the role of Tosca, which I am about to study."

Madame's initial reaction was to say no. She always followed her intuition. When in doubt, don't do it. The final reply was "I'm sorry, my dear one, but I am very occupied at the moment. Maybe at some later date there may be an opening in my schedule."

Regime sounded disappointed when she said, "We will see what the future brings."

"Good-bye for now," said Madame and hung up the phone. She thought, *What a fool that woman is. She was blessed with a big lyric voice and spoilt it by singing Brunhilde. Ternina had told me never to sing Brunhilde as it would ruin me for the great Italian roles.*

Anita reentered the room and said, "Stella called and asked if she could come over and have tea with you this afternoon."

"If she's still on the phone, tell her yes. Three o'clock will be just fine." Madame put on her long mint-green silk dressing gown. "I bought this in Milano. They call it italian green." She looked at her ring, which was the same color. Flashback thoughts of her *Norma* at La Fenice in Venice stirred in her mind. *That house is a jewel box. You don't have to push the voice as you sometimes do at the Met.* She also thought of the Trattoria near the Fenice where she had so many wonderful pastas and wines.

She remembered one particular luncheon with Gian Carlo and the young conductor Thomas, whom he had taken under his wing. Gian Carlo had discussed the possibility of writing on opera especially for her. She had been agreeable, but she realized inwardly that his type of writing was not compatible with her vocal style. They had talked and laughed while chattering about the young Greek American soprano.

"She has a wonderful voice," said Gian Carlo. "I have never heard a voice that big sing coloratura!" He went on to say that she is on some sort of a strange diet and wishes to become a glamour star.

"She had better not take it off too fast or she will develop a wobble in her voice," Madame added.

Gian Carlo then suggested that the three of them take a ride in his speedboat out on the lagoon to the island of Torcello. They all agreed that this would be lots of fun. The trio walked down the long narrow corridors that lead from La Fenice to St. Mark's. The two men, or *boys* as she referred to them, were talking and laughing, seemingly oblivious of her. They were more involved in observing the males along the way than in her at that moment. Oh well, that's the norm in the opera world. She was having a grand time anyway as this presented no problem to her. She was glad to be in their company. At least they are not dreary or sullen.

Madame was attracted to the windows of the shops and glanced at all the glasses, jewelries, and crystals on display. Once in a while she remarked to the boys about a marvelous goblet or piece of silk. Like some apparition, St. Mark's suddenly appeared. She had seen the basilica many times before but always was exhilarated at the sight as indeed she was now.

"Oh look, there are the four houses on the top of the façade to the left."

Gian Carlo said, "Yes. Some claim they date back to the Ancient Greeks."

Thomas added that he thought them to copies, but still magnificent.

Onward, passing the Doge's Palace, her eyes turned past the campanile and focused on the lion atop the pillar. The famous lion is the symbol of Venice. Then, it was over the Bridge of Sighs as they passed the old Hotel Danieli. *What stories that place could tell*, she thought. They finally arrived at the Riva degli Schiavoni, where the boat was waiting.

"Giacomo, bravo! Right here when I need you!" called out Gian Carlo. Madame was introduced to the young fellow who apparently was to pilot their speedboat.

"What an honor, Signora. I have heard many of your recordings. I especially like you as Aida."

"Thanks, darling. It is one of my favorite roles."

She was very attracted to this fellow immediately. He was tall and muscular. The curly blond hair and tan skin were typical of many Venetians. *God*, she thought, *those pants couldn't be any tighter*. He wore the usual blue-and-white-striped shirt. Both of the boys seemed entranced with him. *Maybe he's some type of a hustler*. She thought about this and laughed to herself. *Maybe he's worth it!* Within minutes, they were dashing over the waters of the lagoon. The slight spray of the boat exhilarated her. She turned for another glimpse of St. Mark's and the Church of Santa Maria della Salute, which appeared on the right. They then passed Murano, the island where the creative forces of the Venetians were forged into masterpieces of glass and also many touristic items. She could see the crowds of people descending from the *vaporettos*.

The multicolored houses bind the canals that ran through the island. Thomas remarked that people were moving to Murano to get away from such monstrosities as Mestre. There is even an air-conditioned supermarket there! He showed them some of the small apartment buildings that were being constructed. She thought, *What a pleasant isolation from reality living in such a place would be.*

On they sped. There were men, women, and children walking into the lagoon from the green reeds at the shore. They were having a lovely day. Many were picnicking also. Other boats were passing them along the way. The Italian men stood proudly at the prow, guiding the boats while the women sat in the rear looking glamorous in their bikini suits and sunglasses. *The Italians really love a good time,* she thought. Gian Carlo and Thomas were talking and chatting. Giacomo was almost totally involved in guiding their boat to Torcello.

All too soon the magical ride was over. They pulled on to the side of the dock. "I'll stay here with the boat," said Giacomo.

Madame told the boys to go ahead and that they would meet a little later at the ancient church. She nearly wanted to be alone at this juncture. It was difficult for her to access his reactions to this place. She felt haunted by some unknown ghosts. *I can almost feel them around me*, she thought. There was also an eerie feeling of peace and unreality. There was a long walkway leading toward the large church. Tall green reed-like plants were all around her. She could see the blue-hued water right under the reeds. The slight slap of the water against the side of the road was also eerie amidst the general silence. *Some great tragedy happened here*, she thought. *I feel as if I lived here at some distant time ago.* She had never experienced what some refer to as ESP before and was somewhat surprised at herself. Unable to shake off these haunted feelings, she strode forward. She passed the restaurant on the left. She glanced at the menu. *The prices are dreadful*, she thought.

Being Croatian and from humble beginnings, she was unable to discard a certain sense of pinching pennies. Passing the souvenir shop, she went in but saw nothing of interest. She bought a few postcards. *Oh, there is the church.* She walked in and was immediately possessed by the beauty of the mosaics. She crossed herself and knelt down in one of the pews. Even though at this point in her life she was no longer a faithful Catholic, the sight of the Madonna always moved her. *Oh, there are the boys up in the front.* Thomas, the erudite scholar, was explaining how ancient the mosaics were. She walked up between them and, for some reason, kissed each one of them.

Gian Carlo said, "What's gotten into you?"

She noticed tears in his eyes. *Yes,* she thought, *even the great artistic agnostic is still religious deep inside.* He tried to explain about how the majesty of the figure of Jesus high up on the ceiling had created an ache in his chest. At this point, he just walked away from them and went out the side entrance of the church.

She saw from a distance that he lit a cigarette and took a deep drag from it. "Did you know," Thomas said, "that he is writing an opera about Christmas? He played a scene from it for me the other day. It broke me up. The scene between the crippled boy and his mother would move a stone to cry. It will be a classic someday."

Madame said she couldn't wait to hear some of it. She then took Thomas by the hand and walked out of the church with him. They no sooner were outside when he too lit up a cigarette. "Thomas, I hate to be a nag but you are constantly smoking."

He just looked at her as if to say "mind your own business." Madame was very fond of him. *He really has class, talent, bearing, manners, looks, the works,* she thought. *One of his best characteristics is that he is never condescending and is always kind to those who are not as gifted as he is.*

I wish I had his nobility, but he was born to it, having come from a wealthy American family. He also had the best education money could buy while I came up the hard way. I succeeded only because God gave me a big voice and good luck. Oh well, I should be thankful. Each creature is given his own blessings, and it's up to us to make the most of them.

She couldn't take her eyes off Thomas. *Why am I so fascinated with him? It can't be a sexual attraction as I know that cannot be returned.* However, she stared at the shape of his head. *Beautiful,* she thought, *perfect as a bust of a Roman emperor.* The hair was sandy-brown, fine, and slightly curly. The skin was white, almost porcelain, and the nose and lips were also perfect. She watched as he walked away from her toward Gian Carlo. The walk was firm, graceful, and manly. She always watched his hand movements. *Oh, those hands with long thin fingers and the lovely but not feminine gestures he made. He must be one of the most beautiful creatures on earth.*

However, she shuddered when the image crossed her mind that he probably would not live to be an old man. *Gian Carlo and I are different. We are Mediterranean types, fortunately or unfortunately,* she thought. *Oh, stop this fantasizing and go over to them.*

"Well, boys, shall we go back to Giacomo and the boat?"

"Yes," they said. And off they went. The boat was waiting, and they embarked. Once underway again, the spray of the water seemed to dispel the gloom.

They arrived back at Piazzo San Marco and were all in great humor. Gian Carlo said that Maria, the Greek American, would sing Isolde that night at the Fenice. "She has a box reserved for me. Would you two like to go with me?" he asked.

Both accepted at once. Madame was intrigued at the idea of hearing Wagner sung in Italian.

Only a couple of hours were left before Tristan would commence, so she bade her friends a quick good-bye and headed for her suite at the Gritti Palace. She loved this hotel as the rooms reminded her of an opera setting. *Oh hell*, she thought, *my hair is a mess from the dampness of the lagoon.* She realized that she didn't have time to visit the beauty salon. She hurried to her suite and called the maid to run a hot bath for her. "Pour in plenty of Chanel Oil," she ordered. "Get out my silver-beaded dress." She put this on and then pulled her hair tightly back. "I'll wear that stupid tiara given to me by the deposed Russian countess." She decided to throw a chinchilla wrap over her shoulders and was just about ready to face her entrance. The boys were down in the lobby waiting when she left the elevator.

"Wow," they said, "you are a knockout! Are you sure you are not singing *Tosca* tonight?"

She got a laugh out of this, and the three of them hurried to La Fenice.

The box reserved for them was in the center of the first tier. They entered just as the house lights were dimming so as not to detract from the performance. The longing and surging of the prelude to Tristan soon commenced. Her mind began to wander throughout this lengthy but glorious music. She thought of her girlhood days in Croatia and of her parents and grandparents. She was jolted out of these dreams as the curtain opened and the dialogue between Isolde and Brangaene began. She was indeed fixed on the Isolde, a tall young dark woman rather heavy in stature.

Madame observed her closely through her opera glasses. *The girl is slightly awkward and seems to have some sort of eye problems.* However, the voice was one of the most unusual she had heard. It was big, dark, and piercing, but not beautiful. Madame did get a chill as the famous first-act curse was hurled out at the audience. The voice also had the stamina to ride over the orchestra at the conclusion of act 1. Act 2 went beautifully, as did Tristan's long delirium scene in act 3. The famous transfiguration, or love-death scene, that ends the opera finally arrived. Maria sang in a lyrical, but soaring manner. The conductor, Serafin, came onstage with his Isolde. The audience applauded generously. Madame thought that they were not as generous as a Met audience might have been. *Maybe the Italians are not Wagner buffs*, she rationalized. Gian Carlo thought it only proper that the three of them go backstage to pay their respects. So back they went.

This will be very interesting, Madame surmised. The two, Maria and her aged husband, were giving a small reception in an ornate but intimate salon. The room was highlighted by a beautiful crystal chandelier, Venetian of course. Maria spotted Gian Carlo immediately and walked across the room to greet him. "Caro, mia caro Giani," she called him and kissed him on the cheek. He was his reserved self but embraced her lightly. He probably felt obliged to comment on her performance.

"You brought a new dimension to the role," he said, "especially in your shading of the Italian. Here are my two friends Thomas and Madame."

She, of course, recognized them both. Thomas was by that time already a well-known conductor, and she of course, had been a leading singer for years. Maria had a nervous laugh and a very distinctive speaking voice. Maria spoke to them, in English in a slightly affected manner, watching carefully every word she spoke. Madame took this as a sign that the girl was somewhat insecure.

"Giovanni, please come over," she called to her aged husband. He was many years her senior. The old man dutifully answered her call and slowly approached them. He spoke only Italian and was very courteous. The man seemed absolutely devoted to Maria. She said proudly, "This is my husband, Goivanni Batista."

"Tullio, Tullio," she called. She was referring to the conductor Tullio Serafin. Maria also introduced him to them. *Serafin*, Madame thought, *was the man who really made a great singer out of Maria*. However, at this time, she acknowledged none of this. Serafin then did a very strange thing. He walked over to Madame. Lightly placing his three middle fingers on her throat, he proclaimed the words *bella voce*.

Madame happened to turn her head toward Maria. The girl had a strange love-hate expression on her face. She quickly changed and said in a sort of different higher timbre, "Yes, Madame, you do have a beautiful voice. It is given by God." Madame thought of Maria's Greek Orthodox background. Maria went on surprisingly stating, "That only you and Gigli have this quality. It is natural and of the earth and touches the heart."

No one spoke, as if they all were thinking of her words and of some response. Maria solved the problem with her voice suddenly back to its normal but affected tone. "Let's get on with it," she uttered. "Waiters," she ordered, "bring in the champagne and the food. We're all starving."

Madame grabbed a glass of champagne and gulped it down. She then went to the buffet, which was sumptuous, and partook of the food as did all the others.

CHAPTER II

She woke as if coming out of a trance. *Oh, this old dressing gown, that's what caused it all. Or was it the ring!* She looked at the huge room. God! The ceiling must be twenty feet high, and the windows as well were equally tall. This ancient hotel will never be duplicated. Suddenly, Anita entered and said, "It is three o'clock, and Stella is here. She brought a companion."

"Who is it?" the diva asked.

"She is with the lovely French woman Lily."

"Lily! Oh, I love Lily! Get them each a very dry martini on the rocks with lemon peel. That should relax them until I can pull myself together.

"Lily's here, the little rascal. When she goes on stage, every eye is transfixed on her! She is a true star, and that can't be created by publicity. The audience instinctively knows."

I must try to look halfway decent. She looked into the mirrors and did not like the extra pounds that she observed. The weight seemed to be mostly in the upper part of the torso. She pulled herself into a girdle and a tight bra. *What to wear? What to wear?* She thought of the red silk Chinese Mandarin top with the high collar that Mme Sereni had given her. *I'll wear the ankle-length black flowing skirt under it.* She brushed back her long raven hair and snapped on her rhinestone hair beret.

"Good afternoon, ladies" were her first words as she tried as gracefully as possible to enter the beautiful music room. She deferred first to Lily, kissing her on the cheek. "You look as petite and lovely as ever, Lily. I love that suit you are wearing."

"It is by Chanel," Lily replied.

"Of course, and it's just in from Paris, right?" replied Madame. "Oh, Stella, I can't let you out, my pet." And she also gave Stella a hug and a kiss. Madame asked the ladies to please sit on the mauve brocade couch. She herself sat in her favorite plush red upholstered chair.

"Anita," she called, "bring in the tea and sandwiches." The girls were very giddy from the effects of several dry martinis.

Lily said, "Wait until I tell you about the new baritone who debuted with me last Saturday in *Lucia*. Of course, he has a very fine voice and is very young. I called him into my dressing room before the performance. Do not ever move toward me! I will make all the movements! 'Madame,' he said, 'Believe me, just to be on stage with you will be enough. I will be in seventh heaven.' 'Just sing well,' I replied, 'and look angry! After all, I shall be the Bride of Lammermoor, and you are supposed to be my brother forcing me to marry the wrong man.'"

The two other women laughed. Stella said, "But why, don't you think you were a little mean not to let him make any moves?"

"Well," said Lily, "after he has been on stage twenty-five years, then he can tell people what to do."

Madame added that those days were passing anyway. "I think that in the future, the stage directors will tell everybody what to do. The singers will have no say in it." Stella said, "But that will take away our personality. We shall become mere puppets of the directors." She went on, "Can you imagine some young fag coming over from Italy and telling me what Aida or Mimi are all about?"

Stella then said that she would have to leave. "I have a coaching lesson with that little French Canadian soprano. I'm trying to get her prepared to sing Violetta in *Traviata*. However, even though the poor little one has a beautiful voice, she really doesn't have good high notes. Too bad she sees too much of the Puerto Rican house painter."

They all got a giggle out of this. Stella then left, and Madame and Lily were alone. After the massive front door closed, Lily suddenly walked over to one of the large windows at the end of the parlor. She turned and tears seemed to flood down her cheeks. She appeared about to faint, so Madame half carried her over to the couch.

"Mon petite, what on earth is the matter?"

"What's wrong? I don't know where to start. Lately, sometimes I wish were dead. Maybe, I should go to one of those—oh, how do the Americans label them—'shrinks.' Is that the expression?"

"Yes," replied Madame, "but they don't help anybody. They ply you with tranquillizers and tell you about all your unnatural fantasies."

"We've both had enough fantasy trying to exist in the world of opera." Lily was desperately trying to control herself. "I suppose at my age and after all I've accomplished, I should be better able to cope with what's happening. I can hardly stand it."

Madame made no effort to get the details of her problems. "Just relax there for a while on the couch. Lie back on the pillows and close your eyes. Poor woman, you are all worn out." *I wonder what's bothering her. She usually is bubbling and vivacious. Age can't be the only thing as everyone learns to gradually accept this as part of life. After all, there is only one other alternative.*

Lily suddenly opened her eyes. "All right, I may as well talk to you. I know you are a trusting friend. Pierre has left me. We haven't been getting on for quite some time. He told me he has a very busy conducting schedule and must be constantly traveling. This has been the case for years. His love and affection for me has apparently withered. One must accept these things, I guess. Maybe I should have tried harder to bear him a son or daughter. My career made this difficult. Voice was always one of my prime concerns. So be it. That part of my life is over. My career is soon to end also! Oh, I could go on a few years more, but you know, when I sing in opera lately, I merely seem to be watching the others perform. That feeling of evoking the scared rites of opera has now eluded me. The concert stage has no appeal for me. I am not and never will be a lieder singer.

"There is, alas, one other more terrible problem! My doctor has been giving me certain treatments for cancer. He is trying to bring this dread disease into remission."

On hearing this, Madame could not restrain herself. She went to Lily and held her in her arms as if holding a child. Lily surprisingly pulled away. "Don't pity me. Just try to be understanding as I know you will be.

"The gala to close the old house will be my last appearance. I have decided that money will not be too much of a problem. Pierre has agreed to a financial settlement, and I will be receiving royalties from my recordings. Remember those silly Hollywood movies I made? Now and then, they are revived, and they also play on television. This brings me more income. I think I told you about the apartment I own in Nice.

"France, of course, is the country of my birth. Its culture and language are deeply ingrained into my innermost being."

"Yes," said Madame. "Remember at the end of the war hearing you sing 'The Marseilles' on the radio from Paris. That was indeed a great moment. So, mon petite, what is it that you are planning?"

"This country holds no great allure for me," she answered. "My fans at the opera, of course, are always in my thoughts. They have indeed been wonderful. I feel that they now must become part of the past. The New York apartment is to be dismantled, and the house in Malibu, California, is for sale. When the final Met appearance is over, I shall be finished with America. Nice beckons, and it is there that I shall spend whatever there is that is left of my life. You are, of course, free to visit me at any time. I shall miss you more than is to be described."

Madame tried to express her feelings but could not. She merely embraced her French friend. She suddenly wanted to hear Lily sing once again. "Lily, would you do me a great honor?"

"What is that, my friend?" replied the French woman.

"Would you sing for me before you leave today?"

"I would love you to sing 'April in Paris.' I will play the piano. Yes, I think I can manage," said Madame. She sat down at the keyboard, and Lily started floating the first tones of "April in Paris." Madame listened carefully to every word and note. *The voice is still lovely. It is like an exquisite rose as it first opens from a bud*, she thought. She was very moved and watched Lily in the huge mirror on the wall. There will never be another like her. When the song was finished, she hugged her friend and thanked her for the beauty of her singing.

Lily put on her Chanel jacket to her suit, which she had removed before she sang. Madame told her again of the beauty of her voice.

"Yes, I know, but it is better to leave a season or two too early than a season too late."

"Oh, Lily, you will sing on the day you die."

Lily laughed. "Melba actually did just that. Maybe I'll be like the tenor Laure-Volpe and visit senior citizen homes and sing to aged singers. Oh well, whatever. I told you what I plan, and I am a woman of my word. Well, darling, the time has come for me to leave your beautiful apartment and go home. Lauritz is giving one of his parties next Saturday evening. Why don't you accompany me?"

Madame said, "Of course, my lovely French princess. Meet me here in my apartment, and we will go. It's only two floors away."

Madame watched as the petite French woman walked toward the great doors at the end of the foyer. Anita appeared and opened them for Lily, and she left.

CHAPTER III

Today is the big day, she thought. *It is Tuesday already, and I'm due at Sir Rudolph's office at 11:00 am.* Her images were very diffused at this juncture. *It is not going to be very pleasant, and neither will it be so awful*, she reflected. Desdemona had been a roaring success even though she realized that her singing these days was like playing russian roulette. The voice is tired and wants to go to sleep. It is only because one knows so much about vocal technique that the voice responds at all. It must be warmed up in a certain way. Even then, the results are risky, to say the least. She laughed when she thought of a remark that Jeritza once made. "If I can't sing a high C when I first get out of bed, then I will cancel the performance that evening." *Those were the halcyon days*, she thought. What a grand lady she is! She remembered seeing her at the opera not too long ago. Jeritza was dressed all in black lace with a large black hat over her blond curls. *The skin was still like white porcelain. Jeritza has remained very religious*, she mused, *as she had been accompanied by two priests*. However, Madame recalled that Lotte Lehmann told her that Jeritza was so jealous of her that Lehman didn't appear at the Met until well past her prime. Oh well, these are the vicissitudes of opera!

She looked at the beautiful french clock on her mantelpiece. "Oh god! It's eight thirty already!" She picked up the phone and spoke to Anita. "Anita, tell Igor to have the Rolls Royce at the Seventy-Fourth Street entrance at ten fifteen. He is to take me to the Thirty-Ninth Street entrance of the opera house by eleven am sharp."

"Yes, Madame," she replied.

"Oh, Anita, one more thing, please do not answer the telephone this morning until I return. The critics are not to hear a word of what happens until I can think of my own version of the events. Oh, how they love gossip. Many a career has been ruined by them. Although I myself can't complain. They haven't been so bad to this singer."

She didn't know whether to fuss about her appearance or not. She really detested Sir Rudolph. "He is nothing but a pretentious pig. He wants to appear classy, but that's all a facade. Clever he is, but artistic he is not. Oh well, I may run into some other people while I'm there." She put on a black silk dress and adorned it with the pearls that she bought with the fees from her La Scala appearances. The sable coat will be just fine, and since she didn't have to walk far, she wore her high-heeled shoes. A heavy spray of Givenchy perfume completed the ambiance. Anita gave her the once-over, and nodded her approval.

Through the great doors she went and out into the huge corridors of the hotel. As often happens when one wants to go incognito, she ran into someone. It was Kurt, the famous tenor who lived across the hall. She had sung many times with him, and he was his usual charming self. His career too was nearing its last days. She felt very sympathetic toward him. Recently, some people had booed him at the house. If people don't like a voice, they should stay away. *It's unfair to themselves and the singers,* she thought. That applies to critics also. They have their favorites who always get good reviews. Then there are those who are crucified in the newspapers no matter how well they sing. *I always say, you either like a voice or you don't.*

"Oh, Kurt! Good morning! How is my Rhadames today?"

"I am fine, Madame. You look wonderful," he said.

She said *grazie* but did not dare open a long conversation with him. Her liaison was all too soon to be reality! "Kurt, I'm sorry but I must rush off now. We'll get together very soon as I would love to spend some time with you."

He replied, "Hurry on, my darling. Whoever has the pleasure of your company will be lucky."

She excused herself and pushed onward. She pressed the elevator button and hoped she wouldn't meet anyone else she knew. Luckily, the elevator descended, and the door opened. She mercifully was in the lobby! She managed to get out to Seventy-Fourth Street and saw Igor sitting in the front seat of the Rolls Royce. He spotted her, got out, and opened the rear door for her.

"How are you, Madame?" he asked.

"Igor, you've known me too many years to ask. The answer to that is as complex as the smile on the *Mona Lisa*'s face."

"Madame, I know that you do not often arrive at the Opera at eleven am."

"That is so, Igor, but I do not wish to discuss this problem just now. Just get me down to Thirty-Ninth Street."

"I'll do my best, Madame, if traffic allows it."

She opened her compact for another quick check into the mirror. Vanity is something one never loses even though looks do seem to vanish. *I wish that spirituality would return to my inner self. This preoccupation with age is something that I've always detested. I must replace complete self-absorption with something more positive.*

The limo slowly wound its way down Broadway, past all the famous theaters. They ultimately arrived at their destination. There it was, the Yellow Brewery as some called the old house. It might seem ugly outside, but the red-and-gold interior was still beautifully ornate. What a shame that it is to be torn down. Sir Rudolph says that they need the money to finance the new building. Money can always be solicited. They should make this opera house a national landmark.

The car stopped at Thirty-Ninth Street. Igor got out and opened the door for her. "Igor, I don't know how long I will be."

"Madame," he replied, "I will wait in the garage with the car. Just give me a call when you are ready."

She got out of the car, took a deep breath, and pulled back her shoulders. Walking slowly into the stage door entrance, she was first greeted by the guard. "Good morning, Madame," he said, and there seemed to be a plethora of greetings as the stagehands, dressers, and chorus people spotted her.

Leo, the chorus master, walked over to her and said, "Madame, the chorus is always at their best when you are singing."

"Do you think so, darling?" Madame replied.

He went on. "It is because you can outsing the lot of them."

She laughed at this and suddenly found herself in a very upbeat mood.

Well, here we go, she thought. Sir Rudolph's secretary, Mona Barrington, greeted her as she entered the outer office.

"Good morning, Madame!" she cheerily said. "Would you like something to drink, a martini perhaps?"

Madame laughed at this and said, "Those are only for Mme Flagstad and not this early in the day. She loves them after she sings Isolde. Perhaps, some hot tea would be in order."

Ms. Barrington said she would bring in the tea cart with some assorted pastries. The secretary then lifted the phone and stated that Madame had arrived. The door to the inner sanctum opened, and there was him. He was impeccably dressed in a grey pinstripe suit, with a white shirt and dark blue paisley tie. *Too bad he is sexless*, she thought. *If he were macho, I might do a Tosca-Scarpia scene with him.*

"Come in," he said in his phony British accent, which still bore traces of his Viennese background. "Sit over there near my desk in the red velvet chair."

Just like him to tell me where to sit. He's as arrogant as ever. He sat behind his long empire desk, which indeed looked to be out of the Farnese Palace.

She couldn't help but notice the pictures of Renata and Franco on the wall behind him. Naturally, there was no image of her to be seen. "I like your taste in singers," she said in her deep voice half mockingly.

"What was that, Madame?"

"I mean the pictures behind you."

"Yes, I am fond of them," he answered.

Ms. Barrington knocked quietly at the door and asked if she might wheel in the tea tray. The silver tea set was sparkling, and the Meissen china cups and plates were indeed lovely. Ms. Barrington poured tea for the two of them. She took a sip of her tea and couldn't resist bringing up a matter that bothered her.

"You know, Sir Rudolph," she went on, "this is a grand old opera house. I think it very unfortunate for it to be torn down."

He glared at her as if she was being impertinent. "Madame, I do not wish to discuss matters which do not concern you."

"Well," she said, "I will voice my opinion even over your objections. This is a landmark building with years of tradition behind it. To tear it down to make way for an ugly office building is beyond comprehension."

"I repeat," he said in an angry voice, "the matter is closed. Shall we go on, or is this conference terminated?"

Madame was getting an ego trip out of this and didn't care one iota whether she signed a contract or not. However, she thought of her fans and decided to acquiesce somewhat to the general manager. "Oh!" she said, "these pastries are marvelous." She purposely took a big bite out of one of them.

He continued in a very autocratic manner. "The house will close at the end of next season and will be torn down. The new house will be located farther up town in what will be known as Lincoln Center."

"Yes," she replied, "I have seen pictures of what the exterior will look like. It reminds me of someone's dentures."

"I do not find you humorous. Let us stop this idiotic interplay. You are here only to discuss your contract for next season, if there is a contract at all."

Madame was getting ready to get up and tell the bastard to go to hell, but she was unsure of her financial status and held back her emotions. "Well, Sir Rudolph, won't you go on and explain what I am to sing next year?"

He relaxed somewhat and began to praise her past achievements. Madame thought to herself that she still sold out the house. *The old pig is only thinking of money*, she surmised.

He continued, "I was looking up the annals of this house. My god! You certainly sang, didn't you? Almost five hundred performances, all in the big dramatic parts. You have a magnificent throat. There is no doubt about that."

My, she thought, *he is really pouring on the bullshit*, to corn an American phrase she had learned. "Sir Rudolph, please get to the point. My past history is gratefully acknowledged. We both know that my voice is no longer what it was."

"Yes," he agreed, "but you still drive the audience into a frenzy. Do you want to sing next season or not?"

She toyed with him a little longer. "That depends upon the circumstances."

"What circumstances?" he asked.

"Make your offer!" she imperiously went on.

"Well, even though I loathe the opera, I was going to revive *Andrea Chénier* for you."

Madame replied sarcastically, "But don't the critics loathe that opera also?"

"Yes, we all know that it is in very vulgar taste."

"By *we*," she answered, "you mean those who want to be considered highbrow intellectuals. I myself adore that opera. It is magnificent and stirring. Audiences also find it so. How long can they be bored with Mozart and Rossini?"

Sir Rudolph looked at her with a smirk and a twisted smile. *I know what he is thinking: she is really déclassé and stupid. However, I am the one who will bring the audience to their feet with "La Mama Morta" and the final duet before they cut off my head.*

"My dear woman," he said, "it is really laughable that you could even mention something like *Chénier* in the same breath as *Don Giovanni* or *Barber of Seville*."

"Yes, I know, sir, my breathing is not as it once was."

"That's your problem, not mine. I shall continue with my proposal. There will be eight performances of *Chénier*. You shall be the Magdalena in all of them. Your fee will be as usual."

She stopped him at this point. "By that, do you mean the same fee as is received by Renata and Birgit?"

He replied with a reluctant yes.

She then asked for Franco to be her Chénier.

"No," he said, "Franco wants to sing lighter roles."

"Such as what?" Madame asked.

"Such as Romeo and Werther."

"That is nonsense," Madame said. "He is a real dramatic tenor with a voice as big as a canon."

"Franco will sing what he wants to sing—do you understand? Once again, you are overstepping your domain."

"My domain," she laughed. "I stopped singing Turandot years ago, and while we're at it, why wasn't it offered to me at the Met?"

"Madame, you are being intolerable. However, I shall continue anyway. Richard has already signed to be the Chenier." She liked Richard and agreed. "There will also be a farewell concert to close the house. I would like you and Richard to sing the final duet from *Chénier* at that concert."

"I will gladly do so," she acquiesced.

"Now we are back on the same wavelength." Sir Rudolph sat back and took a sip of his tea. "The contract will be forwarded to your agent. There will be two copies. Please sign them both. He is to send one to me for my records." Sir Rudolph picked up the phone and asked for

Ms. Barrington. "The conference is over," he said to her. "Please come in and escort Madame out."

Madame breathed a sigh of relief and was glad when the door opened. Ms. Barrington reentered the room.

Ms. Barrington then asked Madame, "Are you ready to leave?"

"Darling, I have never been so ready in my life."

The two women then quickly left Sir Rudolph's office. Ms. Barrington quietly closed the door behind them.

"May I use the phone?" said Madame.

"Of course," replied Ms. Barrington.

Madame dialed the garage where she knew Igor would be waiting. She spoke to him and asked that he pick her up at the Thirty-Ninth Street exit of the opera house as soon as possible.

I can't wait to get out of here, she thought. She tossed her sable coat over her shoulders and headed for the exit. Sir George, the Hungarian conductor, was coming toward her down the hallway. *Of all the people, I did not want to see him.*

"Oh, Madame!" he said as he spotted her. She realized that since he was lionized by New York critics, she should say something of praise to him. However, she was not in such a mood. Working with him on *Otello* had been enough for an entire lifetime.

"Good day, Sir George! You may be pleased to note that we will not be associates next season. I will be singing Magdalena in *Chénier*. I am sure you consider that opera to be beneath you."

He seemed surprised. He announced in a haughty manner, "There are other operas I'd rather be conducting. Maybe some other season, Madame." He smiled falsely and headed past her toward the manager's office. *Good riddance*, she thought and really tried to dash to the exit, high heels and all. Thank God! Igor was parked right outside, sitting in the front seat of the Rolls Royce as usual. She was very happy to see him. After those two snobs, it was good to see a human person. Madame always had deep respect for anyone who worked, whether it was a cleaning man at the apartment or, as in this case, the person who drove her car.

"Igor, please drop me off at the Russian Tea Room and then take the rest of the day off." She then laid back into the plushness of the rear seat of the Rolls. There was a sense of exhaustion and tenseness about her.

I really am quite upset, she thought. Soon they reached Fifty-Seventh Street, and she got out at the old restaurant. "See you later, Igor!"

She entered the posh room and was greeted by the maître d' Vladimir. He bowed slightly to her and said, "What can I do for the world's greatest soprano today?"

"You can take me to my usual table in the rear of the restaurant. That's what you can do."

He escorted her to the table. She handed him her sable coat and almost fell into the velvet love seat that was at the side of the table. Vladimir sent a waiter over almost immediately.

"Good afternoon, Madame," he said. "You are looking well. How may I serve you today?"

"Darling, bring me a double martini on the rocks, not much vermouth and with an olive."

"Of course, Madame."

She added, "Bring me also something to nibble on, mixed nuts will be just fine."

Her martini soon arrived, and she felt relieved after the first sip. She hardly had time to reflect when he walked in talking to a friend in Russian. She could hardly believe her eyes when she saw him. *My god! It's Giacomo!*

The beautiful blond hair had grown to his shoulders. He was wearing a dark suit with a white turtleneck sweater underneath. *Should I acknowledge him or not? Better not.* He is with someone else, another man. However, he saw her and walked over to her table.

"Madame, you can't hide from me. I would know you anywhere. Never would I pass by the world's finest artist and not greet her."

She felt happy already. *Compliments will get you everywhere*, she inwardly felt.

"This is my friend Sergei. He is a great choreographer and teacher."

Madame was very curious about the two of them and bade the men to sit down with her.

Giacomo ordered vodka on the rocks for the three of them. She was amazed to see him again and could not associate the present situation with their last meeting in Venice. *I thought he was Venetian, and now he is speaking Russian.* She knew some Russian from her youth in Croatia and had sung Tatiana in *Eugene Onegin* and other Russian parts early in her career in her hometown Zagreb's opera. She never liked prying into other people's business and always preferred them to tell her about themselves if they so wished.

Sergei was the first to speak. He had a heavy accent as indeed did all three of them. English was clearly the second language for the trio.

"Do you care for ballet, Madame?"

"Yes I do," she replied. "It's odd that you would ask," she continued. "Since the last time I was in Yugoslavia, I saw *Romeo and Juliet* with the Bolshoi Company. They were visiting Zagreb. Marshall Tito escorted me personally," she said truthfully, not as one who brags.

Sergei seemed very interested. "What were your impressions?"

"Very positive," she replied. "Especially the Juliet. Her name was Galina Ulanova."

"What about Ulanova?" asked Sergei.

"It is hard to express," said Madame. "She transcended dancing. The power and grandeur of her performance were overwhelming."

Sergei seemed intrigued that she felt the majesty of this work. "What of the music?" he asked.

Madame said she thought the score was one of the greatest of this century. "Especially," she added, "for the scenes between Romeo and Juliet. The tomb scene was also heartbreaking. The orchestration was superb, especially the string section."

"You seem to have a good grasp of the ballet," added Sergei.

"Well," said Madame, "we in opera are frequently associated with dancers since many operas contain ballet. I always admire dancers. They work so very hard. Singers do also, but they are mostly conceited and self-involved."

Sergei and Giacimo both laughed at this. Sergei agreed that dancers do work very hard. They are not paid well as are many leading and overpublicized singers. "Excluding you, of course, Madame!"

Madame replied that she earns every cent. "Do you realize what control and concentration it takes for me to hold that high B pianissimo? I have to walk over the length of the entire Met stage holding onto that note in *La Gioconda*!" she conceded. "I do lean on whoever is playing my mother, La Cieca." Again they all laughed.

"What of Marshal Tito?" Sergei asked.

"Well," she continued and was getting a little tipsy by this time, "the critics have always whispered as have some of my colleagues that I was having an affair with him. I also heard rumors that I was so stupid that only three things interested me in life—singing, sex, and food."

"Is that the order of their judgments?" giggled Giacomo. More laughter. He went on to add that when dancers talk about opera, they often are not so kind.

"What do you mean?" asked Madame.

"Well, for instance, they say the stories are all about the same. For example, boy meets girl, they fall in love, and then later she gets sick and dies or kills herself."

"You both are missing one important element in operatic stories," interrupted Sergei.

"What is that?" they both questioned.

"Religion, of course," said Sergei. "No one can make the sign of the cross on stage as you do, Madame. Especially outside the church on Easter Sunday."

"Yes, Santuzza is a very powerful part. I love to sing her in *Cavalleria Rusticana*. Enough of opera," said Madame.

"I guess you are wondering about me," Sergei then said. "Well, I was born in St. Petersburg. I studied ballet there as a youngster."

"Who were the great dancers at that time?" asked Madame.

"Madame, in my opinion, Pavolova and Nijinsky. The Czar Nicholas and his family visited regularly." He began to sob suddenly. "Why, oh why, did they have to slaughter him and his family in such a brutal manner? The British Crown is to blame. The Czar asked them for asylum and was refused. They were all of the same family. The House of Hanover changed to Windsor in World War I because of their German origin. Never, never will they be forgiven!"

Madame was also moved and replied that no matter who was to blame, their end was their destiny.

Sergei added that the woman who called herself Anastasia was probably a fraud. "Why would they let her go after murdering the others? The grand dowager duchess of the Romanoff family also would not accept her," he said.

Giacomo interrupted to say that there was a fortune in money involved.

Madame again said that destiny would bring out the truth in the end. "Go on about your career, Sergei!"

"Well," he continued, "I was quite a good dancer, but did not have the drive to become a romantic lead. I was, however, an astute observer. I performed many character parts, and gradually, some of the younger dancers came to me for help with their technique. Teaching is a very difficult field. You can tell people how to do things, but whether they grasp or want to grasp what you teach is another matter. There are also personality and psychological factors involved."

"You can say that again," added Madame. "Is Giacomo studying with you?" she asked.

Giacomo interrupted, "Let me tell you, darling. My name is not really Giacomo. I was using that name in Venice trying to earn a living as best I could. You observed me that day, Madame. I'm sure you were aware of what was happening."

She did not reply. What she had on her mind and was soon to become spoken was insulting.

"Don't reply please," he said. "My name is Dimitri. I was also born in St. Petersburg. My parents first migrated to Yugoslavia and then to Venice. You know when you are hungry, you will do anything. Do you know what 'anything' means, Madame?"

"Darling, don't get excited!" She was surprised that he seemed to be getting angry. She laughed a little nervously. "Dimitri—I must get used to calling you Dimitri. That is a very proud name. Remember Dimitri in *Boris Godinoff*?"

"Yes, but I'm not going to be Dimitri to your Marina, am I?"

She laughed again. "One never knows," she said. Madame sensed that things were getting a little bumpy. She thought, *I do not wish to enter into a discussion of his relationship with the two friends, who were my companions in Venice on that lovely day of memories.*

Sergei surmised that both of them were getting uneasy. "You know," he suggested, "I have an idea. My apartment is just across the street. Suppose we go over and have a nightcap?"

Madame was happy to leave the current morass. So was Dimitri.

"Let us go," they all concurred.

CHAPTER IV

The three companions were happy as they stepped out of the old tea room and into the fresh air.

"So where is this nest of yours?"

"I told you and Sergei—across the street."

"There is only Carnegie Hall there," said Madame.

"Well, on top of the hall is where my nest sits."

"I never knew there were apartments up atop the hall," she replied.

They went into the entrance where the Carnegie Recital Hall was and got into a small elevator. The elevator transported them up about six floors. Madame was glad there was no elevator operator as she did not wish to be seen by anyone at this time.

They exited and came to an old iron door, which Sergei opened. "Voila, here is my lair!" He pressed a button and on came a crystal chandelier. The furniture was not attractive. The pieces all looked like they were acquired at a rummage sale. The walls were painted green. They were full of pictures of what appeared to be dancers. There also was a staircase that appeared to lead to another room upstairs.

"Let me take your coat, Madame. My, what a beautiful fur this is. Is it sable?" He continued, "Am I right?"

"Yes," she answered. For some reason, she watched carefully as he hung the garment in the hall closet.

"Shall we sit?" asked Sergei. They did as he requested. Madame took a seat in an old armchair in the corner of the room.

"Dimitri, get us each a vodka double please."

There was a small kitchen off the living area, and Dimitri went to fetch the drinks. He emerged in a few minutes and gave a libation to each of them. "Let me propose a toast to you, Madame. Cheers to one of the world's greatest artists and prima diva del mondo."

"You flatter me." She laughed as they all got up and clinked glasses.

"This is such a joyous occasion," Sergei said. "I never thought when we left here earlier this evening that later I would be entertaining such a noted person."

"Art," she said, "is 99 percent hard work and 1 percent talent."

Dimitri disagreed and said, "Let's face facts. A light church soprano could work twenty years on her voice. She would remain a light soprano. Your voice can soar over a chorus of one hundred! You can also file it down to a floating pianissimo."

"My, Dimitri, you do know voice too, don't you?"

"What did you think," he replied, "I only know about sex?"

Sergei interrupted, "Let's not get into that again."

"Why not?" said Dimitri. "What's wrong with discussing sex? I was a male hustler in Italy, and very well paid at that."

Both Madame and Sergei realized that they all were a bit drunk. Dimitri then said, "Fine, let's have a little fun." He winked at Sergei, as if both knew what was about to happen.

Dimitri then ascended the stairs that led to the upper rooms. Sergei, meanwhile, lowered the lights on the chandelier to dim. He removed his jacket and asked Madame if she would join him on the couch.

What in the world's going on? she asked herself. She had assumed that both of the men were gay but now began to wonder. They are strange; that's for sure. In answer to Sergei's request, she thought, *oh, why not?* She moved over and sat next to him on the couch.

"I am having a grand time," he said, and she agreed. He began to talk of ballet. "Don't you think that its wonderful that Dame Margot has gotten together with the young Nureyev and that they are dancing together? I thought her career was over, but he seems to have breathed youth back into her."

Madame said, "Yes, it's quite a phenomenon."

"Have you seen them dance together?" asked Sergei.

"Yes," replied Madame. "Believe it or not, I saw them in *Swan Lake*. I say that incredulously because I had never seen Dame Margot dance before. To tell you the truth, I didn't expect much. You know, when one knows an artist is no longer young, one assumes that they are not at their best."

Sergei added, "Mme Ulanova certainly refuted that, didn't she?"

"Yes, but the press always tries to destroy everything," said Madame.

"What are their plots all about?"

"I remember that Dorothy Kilgallen reviewed Mme Ulanova in the *Journal-American*. She said that she couldn't dance her way out of a paper bag."

Dimitri laughed and said, "My dear, they were Russian communists, weren't they?"

"Is that why they danced so well?" laughed Madame.

"Of course not," said Sergei, "but prejudice runs very deep. Artists are artists no matter what regimes they are forced to function in."

"Yes, being from Yugoslavia, I know that all too well," continued Madame. "What do you think will happen when Marshal Tito falls?" she asked.

"It will all crumble into civil war," replied Sergei. "There will be wholesale slaughter because of the conflicts between the three great religions—Roman Catholicism, Muslim, and Eastern Orthodox."

"Let's not go on with this," Madame pleaded. "It is all too painful. Can I continue a little further about that night of *Swan Lake*?"

"Of course, angel," he said.

Madame thought, *Well, he is warming up a little*. She went on that she couldn't believe what a beautiful personage Dame Margo presented.

"The arch of her foot alone was a miracle. Her duets with Nureyev were superb. I began to get frightened for her when she had to do those awful repeated turns and pirouettes around the whole Met stage."

"Did she manage?" asked Sergei.

"Well, she seemed to grit her teeth, and with agony and determination, she accomplished them. There was a tremendous roar and applause from the audience. Another thing I remember about that evening was that Jacqueline Kennedy and her teenage daughter, Caroline, were seated right in back of me. Caroline never stopped talking, but her mother told her to be quiet as she had come to see *Swan Lake*, not to hear her daughter chatter."

"I have never seen Mme Kennedy in person," said Sergei. "What did she look like?"

"Well, when she got up during the intermission, I got a good look at her," said Madame. "She was indeed stunning. Tall and thin. She had dark hair, which was all wound up in ribbons. Her dress also was made of silk ribbons. I think the colors were champagne and blue."

"Was she youthful?" asked Sergei.

"Definitely," said Madame. "However, I think the costume was a bit too youthful for her. People were taking pictures of her. I could see the flashes of cameras going off like mad. All of a sudden, men dressed in dark suits appeared from nowhere. They confiscated the cameras and tore out the films. Then they gave them back to their owners. That was quite a night. I will never forget it as long as I live."

All of a sudden, music was heard, quite loud but familiar. After a few bars, Madame recognized that "Salome's Dance" was coming out of the speakers all through the apartment. A spotlight appeared at the top of the stairway. Into this stepped Dimitri dressed as Salome. He wore a bright red wig, which was long and came down over his shoulders. He also wore a long golden cape, and underneath seemed to be yards of chiffon. He did not say a word but gracefully began to descend down the stairway. The movements were beautiful. She couldn't believe her eyes but laughed to herself. She thought, *If only the divas who sang Salome at the Met could move that way.*

Sergei meanwhile inched closer to her. He put his left arm almost around her at the rim of the couch's frame. The music, of course, began building as Dimitri slowly descended the staircase. He was throwing his yards of chiffon down at the two of them. The cape, of course, was also tossed away. He appeared to have his whole body painted gold. By the time he reached the bottom of the staircase, all the outer garment had been torn off. He was concluding the dance in a rhinestone bikini or jockstrap of some kind. Sergei rose from the couch and began to disrobe also. Madame had only one thought now. *Get me the hell out of here!* The two began to dance wildly with each other. Dimitri asked Madame to join them.

"Why don't we all go upstairs and have a threesome?" he asked.

Madame was not interested and remembered where her sable coat had been hung. She made a run for the closet and was out the door before she knew what happened. She slammed the iron door behind her! She buzzed for the tiny elevator. It finally came, and she managed to get down to the street. Happily, a cab was available, and she took it to the Ansonia.

The huge hall at the entrance never looked so good. She walked to the elevator and actually prayed that no one would recognize her. The elevator arrived, and she couldn't find her key; so she rang the door buzzer. Anita came to the door and said, "What in the world happened to you, Madame?"

There was no answer, but the sable coat was almost torn off and dropped to the floor. "I feel drunk," said Madame. "Please take me to my room and put me to bed." Anita dutifully did what her mistress asked.

Madame was soon in her huge bed. Her last words that evening were "Anita, do not disturb me until I awaken. I don't care if the pope himself calls."

Anita closed the doors to the bedroom and left Madame to herself.

CHAPTER V

Morning arrived all too soon. There was indeed a phone call at 10:00 am. It was not the pope, but Sir Rudolph himself. "Good morning," he said. Anita knew the demanding voice at once.

"I must speak with Madame. It is urgent!"

"She is asleep, sir."

"I don't care if she is *La Dormentata di Belezza*. Wake her up!"

"But, sir, she forbade me last evening to wake her."

He relented and added that Madame must call him at his office at 11:00 am. "Very, very urgent business must be resolved."

Anita did not know quite what to say but replied that she would do her best to help him. She wasn't quite sure how to approach the entire situation. Finally, after sitting down and reflecting for a few moments, she made a decision on what to do. *Madame has quite a temper when disobeyed*, she thought, *but Sir Rudolph did sound very perturbed*.

Anita quietly slipped into her mistress's chamber and slowly raised one of the white silk viennese shades covering the window. Sunlight streamed into the room. Madame was wearing the sleeping mask that she usually wore during the night.

"Who is it that dares disturb me?" she muttered. She sat up and pulled a huge pillow behind her head. The diva then pulled off her sleeping mask. She saw Anita standing in front of her huge french provincial bed. "Anita, how dare you wake me?" she said in very deep tones.

"Madame, I know you gave orders not to do so, but Sir Rudolph called a few minutes ago. He said it was very urgent for you to return his call by 11:00 am."

Madame did not seem so angry as had been expected. She simply wanted some hot coffee and a few croissants with butter and jam.

"Yes, Madame," Anita replied. "I shall fetch them at once."

Anita hurriedly left the room to do what was asked of her. Madame slipped once again into her mint-green silk dressing gown. She walked to the huge double-framed gold mirror on her wall. She looked into it.

Diva indeed. I'm beginning to look like a fat old hag. What in the world does that bastard want? Knowing him, it probably has to do with money, she thought. *I must have my coffee before I can function.*

She also had a splitting headache from the events of last evening and, of course, too much drinking.

Well, at least I never smoked cigarettes.

With this, she made the sign of the cross and said a Hail Mary.

Anita reentered with the coffee and pastries.

"Set it down on my dressing table. Oh no!" she added. "I don't want to see another mirror. Set it down near my small settee."

Anita did so, and Madame slowly walked over to her breakfast.

"Anita, please leave the room. Do not answer the phone or answer the doorbell."

"Yes, Madame," Anita replied.

Madame was happy that Anita had brought a nice pot of coffee in her silver pot. There were also extra pastries.

That woman is a marvel, thought Madame. *She always knows what I want. Asking is not a necessity. This coffee tastes wonderful.* "Ah, it is nice and hot!"

She put in an extra lump of sugar and bit into her bun, which was loaded with her favorite apricot jam. She began to feel better and looked at the clock on her dresser. Five minutes before 11:00 am. This is really going to be something!

Anita called the opera house on the other phone. "Tell Ms. Barrington that I wish to speak to Sir Rudolph. I shall accept the call in my boudoir."

In a few minutes, Anita buzzed her and said that Sir Rudolph was on the phone. With great trepidation, she picked up the receiver. He was the first to speak.

"Good morning, Madame. Thank you ever so much for returning my call."

He went on almost without taking a breath. "A great crisis has hit the opera!"

She couldn't imagine what he was going to say. "Go on, Sir Rudolph, what is this crisis?'

He responded, "Mme Rinaldi's mother has died! She is heartbroken and already has taken the body on an Alitalia jet home to Milano."

"Oh, that poor woman!" exclaimed Madame. "They loved each other so much, and now it is all over. She will not be able to sing for a long time."

"Precisely," said Sir Rudolph. "The crisis now at the opera is that she was to have sung *Aida* at next Saturday's matinee broadcast. I have called Mme Maria Curtis Verna, her understudy. She refuses to replace her. She was in tears herself and told me she didn't feel well enough to face Rinaldi's huge and disappointed fan club."

"Madame, I will pay you anything within reason to help us in this dire emergency."

Madame cleared her throat as she did not know how to respond. "I must think this over, Sir Rudolph," she uttered.

He said, "Please, Madame, you are such a great artist, and the public adores you. You must do us this favor."

While he was speaking, ideas began forming in her mind. *I, of course,* she mused, *was the greatest Aida. There were high pianissimos for the "O Patria Mia" and the power to ride over the chorus in act 2. Alas, I can no longer do this."*

"Madame, are you still there? Please converse with me. I'm desperate."

"I cannot replace Renata in *Aida*. That is impossible. I am a great star. A star does not dim her luster by becoming an understudy. However, as one of your leading Italian divas, I may go on next Saturday."

"You are as difficult today as you were in my office last week."

"Sir Rudolph, do not forget that it is you who called me and are asking for favors."

"Get on with your proposal, Madame. What are your terms?"

"I wish to sing my first Met *Tosca*. That is what I want! *Tosca* has been mounted for me at La Scala, Covent Gardens, and in Paris. You, however, never asked me. I was always the workhorse for the big Verdi roles, which your favorites chose not to sing."

There was a long pause. Sir Rudolph finally continued, "All right, *Tosca*, so be it! I'll try to get Mario or Franco to sing opposite you."

"That will be just fine," Madame went on, "but who will sing Scarpia?"

"Well," said Sir Rudolph, "a young baritone named Sherrill was to have sung Amonasro. He has a great voice and is very handsome! I am sure he can do the Scarpia. In fact, he has already sung it at that horrible opera company on Fifty-Fifth Street."

"We shall see," said Madame.

"There will be a piano rehearsal tomorrow at eleven am with Professor Weigert. You must attend. I will arrange," he continued, "for the set of act 2, to be put up on Saturday morning so that you can find your way around."

"*Va bene*, Sir Rudolph. I'll see you tomorrow. Oh!" she added. "I shall wish double my fee and also my usual contribution from RCA Victor. Please discuss all of this with my agent. I shall have no time for such trivia."

"Yes, Your Highness," he sarcastically said. "Good-bye for now," he added and hung up the phone.

Madame was in a state she didn't quite know. This has come as a complete surprise. *So the bastard still respects me. I'm the only one he trusts to take over the audience after such a tragedy! I must be proud of myself after all these years. I think I'll call Stella and talk this over.*

She buzzed for Anita, who responded right away.

"Anita, please call Stella. See if she is at home. If she is, let me speak to her. Thank you, darling," she said.

Anita managed to reach Stella and promptly transferred the call over to Madame.

"Stella, I have something sensational to tell you!"

"You don't have to," said Stella. "I already heard that you are to sing *Tosca*."

"How in the world did you find out?"

"Well, I shouldn't repeat this, but Ms. Barrington called me about another matter and happened to tell me of your little secret." She laughed as she spoke.

"It is sort of ridiculous at this stage, isn't it?" Madame also began to laugh. "Stella, you've got to help me with this. I haven't sung *Tosca* in years, even though I was bragging to Sir Rudolph about my past success in the role."

"What can I do for my dear lady?" Stella asked.

"Please come over. I must go through the score with someone. You are the only one I can trust."

"What time is it?" asked Stella.

"About noon," responded Madame.

"Well, I'm hungry. I haven't had lunch yet," added Stella.

"Jump into a cab and get over here. I'll have Anita prepare some pasta for both of us."

"Fine," responded Stella. "I'll see you in about one hour."

"Anita!" she called, and the faithful woman was in the salon within minutes. "Please prepare some lunch. Stella will be here soon, and I wish her to have something good to eat. Make a greek salad with plenty of tomatoes, feta cheese, and anchovies. Then prepare some spinach fettuccini with bolognese sauce. Send down for some cannolis for dessert. Thanks, angel. I know how Stella loves to eat. She can't think until after lunch, and I need her expertise desperately at this juncture."

She went over to the piano and began to hum a few scales. *Well, the voice feels all right.* She had great faith in the *voce chiuso*, which she had learned from Emma Calvé.

You sing with the mouth closed, and it places the voice. Only Lily and Richard have the nerve to use this on stage when they get in vocal trouble.

She went over to the bookcase where all her scores were kept. *God, look at all those Verdi scores. They made me do all the Verdi roles because no one else wanted to sing them. Ah! Here is Puccini,* Boheme, Butterfly, Turandot—and finally, she pulled out La Tosca. *I had sung them all when I was younger and thinner. Mozart too. Yes, my Donna Anna was considered by Bruno Walter and Toscanini to be one of the best. The Met never asked me to do this either. I guess I'm only a workhorse. The bastards. But I have to make a living. What a goddamn rotten way to make money. I'll be glad when I can retire and get away from the whole charade.*

She heard the phone ring. Anita picked it up. "It's Stella," she said.

"Well, tell the door people to send her right up." *Thank God for Stella!*

In a few minutes, Stella arrived. She hugged Madame and said, "Well, they do need the old girl, don't they?"

"Let's not dwell on age," said Madame. "I have to think now of myself as a young girl in love with Mario and ready to kill for him."

"Sounds like even fun to me," said Stella.

"We'll see later how much fun it is when you start taking me through the role," said Madame.

Anita announced that lunch was ready.

"I think we will eat in the kitchen, okay? It will be easier for Anita."

"Fine," said Stella.

She told her what lunch would consist of and asked Stella if she would like some wine.

"Chianti would be super good," said Madame, "but we can't drink too much before *Tosca*." They both laughed again.

The lunch was delicious, and they did drink a little too much of the strong red Chianti. Well, into the huge music room they went.

"Where do you want to start, Stella?"

"Well, let's talk a little first, Madame, if you don't mind."

Madame nodded her approval.

"*Tosca* is not a bel canto role, as you know. Even with a dramatic voice such as yours, there are certain danger zones. The first act is no big deal. Just be cuddly with Mario and very aristocratic with Scarpia. If he is handsome, you can be a little flirtatious.

"The second act is another matter," continued Stella. "Once the door to Scarpia's room in the Palazzo Farnese closes behind you, things get very rough vocally and histrionically. There are several high Cs, and they must be sung. In the off-stage cantata, at the beginning of the act, there is a chorus with you.

"However," Stella then interrupted, "let us go over to the piano. I wish to illustrate something to you. See here where Scarpia taunts you and sings 'Che ad ogni.' (He'll answer in blood for every wrong answer you reply. No, no, you instrument of Satan!) You must up go to a forte high C and then descend into the lower range in chest voice."

"Stella, I am well aware of this. I've done this before!"

"Yes, my darling, but that was years ago. A few pages later, there's another high C, but not so dangerous. You do not have to go down to the chest voice afterwards."

"You talk as if these high notes grow on trees," said Madame. "Maybe I should have done *Aida* after all." Madame was getting annoyed at Stella and herself. "Why did I ever get into this whole damn thing? Oh well, I can't get out of it now."

Stella saw that Madame was perplexed. "I'm only preparing you for the 'Vissi D'Arte'! That's it! The audience only worries about what we previously discussed if your voice cracks on the high notes.

"The aria is another matter. You can bring down the house if you can sing it beautifully after all that screaming. There's almost dead silence before you start it. Start softly if you can. You still have a lush middle range, so don't be afraid to sing full during the rest of the aria. Sing a powerful high B flat at the climax 'perché, signor.' Then on the next 'ah, ah,' pull the voice back to pianissimo. Finish in full voice."

"You do know all the tricks, don't you, Stella." Madame laughed and said, "You sing quite a Tosca yourself! You better get ready if I get sick."

"I'm sure you'll manage very well, honey," said Stella. "We'll see to that, won't we?"

"Let's get on with it then."

The two women spent several hours going through the score. Both were wet with perspiration at the end and hugged each other. Madame rang for Anita. "Stella, I could use a drink. How about you?" Stella nodded yes!

Anita entered the salon. Madame said, "Bring a pitcher full of martinis on ice. Make some of those little kosher franks wrapped in pastry. Get them in here as soon as you can."

"Yes, Madame," Anita replied and left for the kitchen.

Stella said, "Madame, do you really think this is going to be a success or a big fiasco?"

Stella replied that she thought *tutto va bene*. All goes well.

Anita had faithfully brought in the drinks and snacks.

"Let us toast to your success," said Stella.

Madame said, "No, let's drink to each other. I would never do this without your wise counsel. One must have someone to have faith in and confide in, especially in the rat race called opera."

"Honey," said Stella, "after all these years, you must know what this is all about."

"Yes, I think I do, but it's always terrifying going out before thousands of people. Even though some adore you, one never knows with the voice. It may not always obey! Thank God I am quite fluent in Italian. At least I know what I'm singing about."

Stella said, "Try to think much more of the play and your role as a singing actress. You've spent years spinning out pianissimo high tones, but as Tosca, you will be expected to act as well."

Madame concurred as she was sipping her drink. "After all, verismo is verismo." Stella laughed and said, "*Vero, vero.*" (That's true.)

The two women laughed and chatted for a long time until dusk began to descend on what Stella referred to as the Piccolo Palazzo (small place).

"Well," said Stella, "honey, you had better rest now for tomorrow's rehearsal."

Madame said, "Oh, I'm not looking forward to that at all, but I guess you are correct."

Stella gave her a kiss on the cheek and bade her farewell and good luck regarding the next days' events. Madame rang for Anita. The maid entered the nurse chamber promptly. "Please get Stella's coat. Call Igor and tell him to take her home safely and promptly."

"Yes, of course, Madame. I will." Anita escorted Stella out quickly. She saw that Madame was very tired.

Left alone, Madame once again gazed into the mirror. *I'm too old for all this nonsense*, she thought. *After it's over, what will I have to live for? I guess I'll just do the best I can.*

She went into her boudoir. She also rang again for Anita. Anita returned quite breathless. "Madame, I just finished taking Stella downstairs and put her into the Rolls Royce. I also gave Igor your instructions."

"You are an angel as usual. Please help me undress." Madame was somewhat overwrought. "Please get me my sleeping pill and some water. I know I shouldn't after drinking, but I must sleep now."

After taking her pill and a glass of water, Anita helped Madame climb into her huge french bed. She covered her with a white quilt, and off to sleep she went.

CHAPTER VI

Thursday

Anita was awake early the next day. She had a sense that everything this morning would be difficult. She went into the kitchen to prepare a brew of hot coffee. Shortly afterward, at about 8:00 am, the phone rang. *Oh god*, she thought, *who would call at this hour? If only it's the wrong number.* The phone rang five times before she picked up the receiver.

"What the hell is wrong?" a familiar voice said loudly. Anita recognized Stella's tones at once.

"Madame is in deep slumber," said Anita, "and I presume that you must speak with her."

"Why the hell do you think I'm calling?" Stella asked. "I know she's sleeping, but there are a few matters I must discuss with her." Stella continued, "I'll tell you what. I'll hang up for now. She will be bitchy, but wake her and tell her to call me back pronto." Anita was not in a good mood either and felt like saying "Why don't you come over yourself and wake her up?" Instead, she was as dutiful as ever and said, "Certainly, Mme Stella. I will do my best to get her up."

Oh mercy, thought Anita, *she will be annoyed when I wake her. However, her nibs must be down at the opera house by eleven am for rehearsal anyway.* With great trepidation, she opened one of the huge doors to Madame's sleeping chamber. Madame was fast asleep under her covers as Anita had left her the night before. There was one exception, however. She had put on her black sleeping mask!

Anita did not speak. She merely slowly drew open the viennese curtains on the window opposite the bed. Madame, of course, wasn't completely disturbed by this because she had on her sleeping mask. However, she did hear some sound of movement, and she turned over and groaned.

Anita stood at the foot of the bed. Madame suddenly sat up, pulling up a pillow behind her at the same time.

She almost tore off her sleeping mask and said to Anita, "Once more you disturb my rest!" As she cleared her throat, Madame seemed to realize that today was rehearsal time for *Tosca*!

"Oh, Anita, is it really that hour already?" she asked.

Anita went on that it was only shortly after 8:00 am, but that Stella had already called and said that Madame was to call her back very soon.

"What in the hell does she want?" said Madame. "We went over everything yesterday afternoon."

"She didn't tell me, Madame," added Anita.

Madame didn't wish to interrogate Anita any further. She merely asked her to bring her a small pot of coffee with some cream.

"Yes, Madame," responded Anita. "I have already made some."

I can't call Stella until I have some hot coffee. I'm still exhausted from yesterday, she mused.

Anita soon came in with the hot coffee as requested.

"Set it there next to my bed like the angel you are."

Anita did as her mistress bade. "Anything else, Madame?"

"No, dear," Madame replied, "but be close at hand. I shall need you."

"Yes, Madame," retorted Anita.

Madame rolled herself higher back onto her pillows. She began to sip the hot beverages, and with each sip, she began to feel more awake.

There is no rest for me now. Stella wouldn't call me unless there was something to worry about. No, she thought, *it's not to do with music. There must be some other problem.*

She finished her coffee and almost dragged herself out of the bed. As she did so, she felt an ache in her back. *Age is surely a curse. This damn weight isn't helping me either. Oh, where is that green dressing gown? There it is on the chair on the other side of the room.* Anita had evidently placed it there with her slippers underneath.

Madame walked across the room, refusing to look into the large wall mirror as she passed by. She got into her gown and slippers and rang for Anita.

Anita soon appeared. "Yes, Madame?" she asked.

"Get Stella on the phone, I'll pick up the receiver in here. Thanks, darling," said Madame.

Within five minutes, the phone rang. Madame picked up the receiver. She knew Stella's voice at once.

"Good morning, angel," said Stella.

"I'm no angel," replied Madame. "I feel more like Mephisto this morning. Stella, please get on with it." She almost pleaded. "What has gone wrong now?"

Stella said, "Nothing has really gone wrong. I just wanted you to be ready for something."

"Ready for what, Stella?"

Stella went on to say that Mona Barrington called her last night to relate that Sir Rudolph had released quite a story to the press.

"What?" said Madame. "Why is he making a big deal out of this?"

"That, I don't know, but Ms. Barrington told me quite a bit."

"A bit of what?" asked Madame.

"Well," Anita went on, "Thomas will conduct the *Tosca*, and Sir Rudolph has asked Sir Tyrone Guthrie, the famous English director, to stage the performance."

"That's impossible," raged Madame. "I'm not a little marionette to be pulled around on strings! Do they think they can make me into a singing actress in two days? All of these sirs! Sir Rudolph, Sir George, and now Sir Tyrone! Has the Queen nothing better to do than to torture a simple woman?"

Stella could not help but laugh and added, "You are as simple as the ocean is deep."

"Whatever your opinion of the matter does not annoy me." Madame added, "You said earlier that I should get ready for something. Would you please make me aware of what your diabolical mind has conjured up?"

"Well," laughed Stella, "now you're projecting your insecurity onto me—aren't you, my dear angel?"

"Stella, please stop torturing me. You are not a very good Scarpia, anyway."

"Wrong register, my dear. However, I will now inform you of what to beware of," Stella continued. "When you step out of the hotel, the paparazzi will be there. I have no doubt about that. Therefore, you better pull yourself together in more ways than one!"

Madame retorted sharply, "You mean, wear a tight girdle and smile, right?"

"Right," said Stella. "The tabloid slaves no doubt will be popping their cameras at you."

"This is ridiculous. I was never a glamour queen before. Now at the end of my career, I'm supposed to become Maria!"

"Yes, and what's more, I hear that people are fighting to get to see you as Tosca!"

"Honey," said Madame, "I get the picture. I don't wish to speak any further as I don't want to be hoarse for the rehearsal!"

"Okay," said Stella, "but don't say I didn't warn you. Bye now, angel."

"Au revoir," concluded Madame and hung up.

Madame thought for a few minutes. *I should be upset, but I'm getting more and more excited.*

She then dared to walk over to the long wall mirror. *Ah, to transform this hag into the beautiful and sensual Tosca. That will require some doing! Maybe I can invoke the fairy godmother from the* Wizard of Oz *to wave her magic wand over me.*

She began to laugh very loudly, so much so that Anita rushed into the room. "What on earth is wrong, Madame?" she asked.

"What's wrong? Everything is wrong. I should have never gotten into this whole rotten mess. That damned bastard, Sir Rudolph—it's all his doing! Money, money, money—that's what he's thinking of!"

"Stop screaming, Madame," said the worried Anita. "You'll have no voice left for rehearsal."

"The rehearsal," Madame went on. "Wait until the critics hear the performance. They will rip me up to shreds. I, however, intend to fool them by whatever means I still have at my command. Anita, you must now help me to get ready. What shall I wear do you think?"

"Basic black's always the best," said Anita.

"You are right, Anita, as usual. Get out my black moiré dress with the skirt below the knees. Even though my legs are not ugly, as are those of some divas I know, I wish to be very dignified. Since Sir Tyrone will be directing me, bring out my La Scala pearls. I shall adorn myself with them. I must wear, thank God, cuban heeled shoes as Mario is sure to ask me not to wear high heels.

"You know that he wears lifted sandals as Rhadames to make himself look taller. I'm sure the only thing he will ask me is 'What kind of shoes will you wear as Tosca?'"

Anita exited the boudoir, and in five minutes, she returned. "Here is the black moiré dress and also the black cuban heeled shoes."

Madame at the juncture was struggling to get into a corset. Anita was surprised at this since she had expected Madame to wear a bra and girdle.

"No, no, Anita," said Madame. "I know what you're thinking, but a bra and girdle do not control a bulging midsection. Come over here to me, Anita. See those strings in back of the corset? Pull these as tightly as you can."

Anita, indeed, began tugging at the strings. *Who does she think she has become*, thought Anita, *Scarlett O'Hara?*

"Making an old woman look young is always a chore," huffed Madame, "but what is . . . is. Get the dress now."

She had not worn it in a while and thought that she might not get into it. Anita helped her to pull the garments over her head, and by God's mercy, the diva still fit into it.

Madame asked, "What color stockings shall I wear?"

Anita replied that black would be fine.

"Very well, fetch them for me," said Madame.

Anita went to the lingerie cabinet and brought out a pair of light black cotton stockings.

"Why not silk?" asked Madame.

"Because number one, cotton will be warmer, and number two, you may be thrown around a lot in the second act."

Madame was surprised at Anita's astuteness and said, "Anita, you never cease to amaze me."

Anita also added, "You had better take a cardigan sweater along. You know how drafty the Met is."

Madame then walked over to her dressing table. The dresser had three mirrors—one large one in the middle and two smaller ones on either side. There were also lights around the mirror, which had not been turned on in years. Anita was therefore surprised when Madame suddenly switched on the lights.

"There," she said, "let us see what we are looking at."

"Oh, Anita, couldn't you just cry. Look at this wreck of a face."

Anita did not know how to reply as any reply would be the wrong one. Anita took out a brush and began to brush her mistress's hair.

"I think you should wear it straight back, and I will place a rhinestone beret over the crown of your head."

Madame simply nodded approval. She began to look better already. She thought, *this girl is so good to me that I must place her in my will.* "I don't wish to be too made up, Anita, as it is daytime as you well know."

"I think that some light tan pancake makeup will be fine along with eyebrow pencil and a little mascara. Okay, Anita?" asked Madame.

"Fine," said Anita.

Madame began to apply her own makeup. "Go and bring me my pearls, darling," she requested. "You know that the La Scala management had fondly given them to me after a series of *Normas* I sang there years ago."

"Yes, Madame," replied Anita.

By the time Anita had brought the pearls, Madame had finished with her makeup. Anita said, "Pardon me, Madame, but don't you think your artificial pearls would do just as well? You don't know what situations you will encounter down at the opera house."

"Yes, yes, Anita, you are right. Why cast pearls before swine."

Anita laughed and thought, *She really loathes Sir Rudolph.*

"Anita dear," Madame continued, "Please go to the large armoire and get out the leopard coat and hat. They were given to me by President Nasser after I sang *Aida* outside the magnificent ruins of Luxor. Oh, that was some occasion. You really must visit Egypt someday, Anita. The pillars of the temples are gigantic. I can't imagine a more perfect setting for any *Aida*."

Anita replied, "Are you going to pay for it?"

Madame gave her a terrible look. "My dear child, that is the first time you snapped back at me."

"Sorry, Madame," said Anita but thought to herself, *she really is raving today!*

"Nonetheless, bring me the coat." Madame had not worn the furs for years. Anita soon brought in the leopard-skin coat and hat.

Madame was now standing with her shoulders pulled back and stood right in front of the full-length mirror.

"How do I look, my dear?"

"Wonderful, Madame." The corset did seem to make her look much thinner and pulled in the waistline area. "Here, Madame," Anita continued, "I will help you put on the fur coat."

Once the coat was on, she seemed to take on a sort of magisterial look. "Now, please place the pillbox matching hat on the top of my head. There, my girl, what do you think?"

Anita was impressed and also moved by the appearance of her mistress. She really is going all out. This probably will be her last appearance as a grand diva.

The phone rang. Madame picked up the receiver.

"It is Igor. You must leave very soon if you are to make it down to the opera house by eleven o'clock." He added, "I have hired a Pinkerton guard to go with us. The guard will be up there in five minutes to escort you down. I will have the Rolls Royce outside the Seventy-Third Street exit."

"Igor, I cannot argue with you. I never do, but is all this fuss necessary?"

"Yes, Madame, I definitely know. I have been snooping around downstairs. The reporters are waiting. There are quite a few, and they have cameras. I do not want them to push you. I cannot control the car, them, and the driving all at once."

"Yes, yes, darling, send up the guard. I shall be ready." And she hung up the phone. "Anita, Anita," she called, "One more thing, bring me my dark glasses."

Anita did so. Madame quickly put them on along with a generous puff of Christian Dior perfume.

The doorbell rang.

"Here I go, Anita!"

Anita ran over and gave Madame a kiss and a hug. "You will be just fine," she said and ran to open the door. A good-looking tall man in a gray uniform was there.

"Darling," said Madame, "hold my arm tightly and guide me downstairs."

She could hardly see through her dark glasses. "What is your name, handsome?" she asked.

"Patrick."

"You must be Irish," she said with a smile.

Somewhere along the line, he went on, "I had Irish blood."

"Look, Patrick, when we get to the street exit with my chauffer Igor will be waiting, I will hold on to you for dear life. Just get me into the backseat of the limo. Push me in if you have to. As you can see, I am neither petite nor young. Then jump in beside me in the rear seat."

"Got everything, lady?" said Patrick.

The elevator arrived; they entered, and soon they were down to the lobby. The doorman had succeeded in keeping the wolves at bay. However, Madame could see them through the windows of the revolving door.

"Lady, you go first. I'll be right behind you."

Madame felt like a movie star as she stepped out into the street. She was glad that she wore her dark glasses as the flash bulbs were popping all around her. Patrick was right at the back of her.

Since he was a big fellow over six feet tall, the paparazzi didn't push into them. Madame just stood still, held up her right arm, which was incased in a big black glove.

"Boys, please. Take all your pictures now and then be done with it."

She smiled graciously for the cameras. Of course, there were plenty of questions being tossed at her.

"Are you afraid of replacing Rinaldi?"

"Why did you not sing the *Aida*?"

"How come you want to sing *Tosca* at this stage?"

Madame was enraged at this question and then said, "That's it, boys." She looked back at Patrick and ordered, "Push me through these idiots."

Igor had the Rolls at the curb, with the rear door open. Patrick used some rough language and also a few jabs to get her into the car. Once there, both he and Igor managed to get her inside. Patrick jumped in beside her, and Igor took form at the front driver's seat behind the wheel.

The paparazzi were still taking pictures and peering in the windows as the huge Rolls Royce took off for Thirty-Ninth Street and the opera house. Igor was doing his best getting down Broadway through the many traffic lights and dense traffic. Patrick looked into the rear window and saw them being followed by other vehicles, probably the paparazzi.

Madame was having fun. "I haven't been getting this much attention in years." She laughed and turned to Patrick. "Handsome, let's give the boys something to crow about. Why don't you give me a big kiss so they can all see?"

"Lady," he said, "you're crazy. Bodyguards aren't paid to do that."

She answered, "So what, do as I say. I'll pay extra."

"Lady," Patrick answered, "I only kiss dames if I want to." He suddenly grabbed her and gave her a full kiss on the mouth, a long one at that.

"Darling, you are taking my breath away. How will I be able to sing *Tosca*?"

"I don't give a damn about that crap," he said, "but you are quite a woman."

Madame started wishing that the journey would take longer as she wasn't looking forward to the rehearsal at any count.

However, Igor, the ever-faithful one, soon pulled up outside the Thirty-Ninth Street entrance of the opera house. Patrick jumped out and opened the door for her. The paparazzi were of course there taking pictures. Madame pretended to be annoyed but smiled graciously.

Sir Rudolph suddenly appeared outside the door. He was in a very authoritative and aristocratic mood.

"Gentlemen!" he called out loudly. "Stand back and let this great singer pass into the portals of song. If you behave yourselves, there will be a photo op session right here outside of the house. No one will be admitted during the rehearsals, except the participants.

The reporters seemed impressed by his European-style discipline. They backed off to the side, and out stepped Sir Tyrone, Thomas, and the new baritone Sherrill. Mario was nowhere to be seen. Sir Rudolph asked Madame to be at his right side and the others around them.

"Now, gentlemen, you may take photos. When I give the word, you will snap your pictures. When I say leave, you will leave or be arrested for trespassing. I repeat and reiterate, the police are on their way. That's it, do you understand?"

The paparazzi nodded agreement and seemed somewhat in awe of this Austrian-born but tilted Englishman. There were many flashes, and Sir Rudolph raised his fist and said, "Basta! That's enough, it is finished!" The police did appear and ordered the press to leave.

Madame told Igor to go and wait for her with Patrick. "I'll call you later as usual," she informed him.

The party finally entered the hallowed halls of song. People were running about, and there seemed to be a buzz of excitement all around them.

There were conductors, coaches, assistant conductors, chorus members, and others milling around the corridors. Everyone nodded and smiled to Madame as she walked toward the stage.

She was surprised that Sir Rudolph was leading the group toward the main stage. He suddenly stopped and said, "This rehearsal is to be held onstage. There will be no scenery or orchestra. The rehearsal is to be a making rehearsal. Only Professor Weigert will play the piano. Thomas will conduct, and all of you will follow the directions of Sir Tyrone to the letter."

Madame squared her shoulders as if she were marching into battle.

Sir Tyrone then said, "If I may, I would like to see Madame alone for a little while."

"All right," said Sir Rudolph, "but not for long. Time is of the essence now."

Sir Tyrone then took Madame off to one of the adjacent rooms. They entered the room, and Sir Tyrone closed the door behind them. "My lady," he said to her, "that man is a pain in the butt. I only agreed to this because of the star attraction."

Madame seemed surprised at this remark.

He went on, "I have admired your voice and artistry for many years. Of course, in such a short time, I cannot presume to tell you how to act. You have your own mannerisms, and the audience knows them. Sincerity and feeling are your attributes on stage, and you are every much prima donna, and all are aware of this. That tyrant Sir Rudolph is only using my name for prestige. I, of course, like the money and the publicity this will bring. The suggestions I make will come as we go through the score."

Madame said, "I have seen some of the plays you have directed and also admire your work. I think that we two shall get on just fine."

"That's it then," said Sir Tyrone.

"Shall we rejoin the others?"

"Fine," said Madame.

It was indeed chilly when they arrived onstage. Madame threw the gray knit sweater that Anita had given her over her shoulders. Madame knew Professor Weigert quite well.

He was a fine pianist and coach. His wife was quite a well-known Wagnerian soprano. Madame had heard him working with this fine young singer many times while she was busy working on the Italian repertoire at the house. She therefore had confidence in him and liked him. He had often smiled at her when passing through the building.

Why, though, did Sir Rudolph assign him to play the rehearsal? Probably, she thought, *because of his scholarly and strict to-the-letter musical discipline.* Sir Rudolph was among them all too soon. He beckoned them to gather at the piano.

"Where is Mario?" he roared.

"He is always late," the wardrobe mistress responded.

"Where is Signor Mario?" Sir Rudolph demanded.

"He is down in the costume area prancing around," he replied.

"I suppose he is showing everyone what a grand physique he has," added Sir Rudolph. With that he ran offstage to the phone. Everyone could hear him screaming.

"Tell Mario to get his ass up here, Schnell. I mean fast," said Sir Rudolph.

In a few minutes, Mario appeared looking as handsome as ever. Madame couldn't help but laugh when Mario came over to her and whispered in her ear, "Please don't wear high heels at the performance."

So they all were there finally, including the young baritone Sherrill.

Sir Rudolph went on. "Let us commence."

Professor Weigert took his seat, and Thomas came out and stepped in front of the piano.

Sir Tyrone took control and started moving them around the stage. "Imagine that you are in Rome and inside a magnificent basilica. Go on, Mario," he said, "and become Mario Cavaradossi. You still mount a platform and are painting a beautiful woman."

Mario was soon singing the first tenor aria, "Recondita Armonia." Madame could not take her eyes off Mario. He looked marvelous as he began to pour out his great voice. She had thought everyone would be singing softly, but Mario sang full voice. He had told her many times of his lowered larynx vocal technique. This enabled him to sing very loudly, but to the chagrin of the critics, Mario had trouble singing sotto-voce.

Gigli had also discussed his vocal technique with her years earlier. He remarked that the critics all thought he was in poor taste because he was always sobbing while singing. Little did they know Gigli was using this method of emission to relax his throat.

He did have the loveliest tenor voice I had ever heard, recalled Madame.

Suddenly, Sir Tyrone called out. "Bravo, Mario, now you descend the platform and go to meet your Tosca. Madame, you come on from stage left and greet your lover." Madame was soon swept up into the duet with Mario. She also sang full voice, somewhat to her surprise.

I should be saving myself, but I've got to see what's left of my voice.

Soon Mario departed, and she was left alone with Scarpia.

The young man before her as Scarpia was truly a find. Tall, blue eyed, and with sandy brown hair, he looked like a cowboy right in from the West.

Too bad this is not Fanciulla. He'd make a great Jack Rance, she mused.

Back to *Tosca*, it all became like a dream. Madame was actually enjoying herself.

"Now, Sherrill, put out your hand. Pretend it is filled with water," said Tyrone. "Madame, take the holy water from his hand and make the sign of the cross with it as only you can."

So they went through the entire *Tosca*. Madame was especially pleased with act 2. She had strong vibrations about this young Scarpia. The mixed emotions he aroused in her enabled her to feel her way into the part as she never had before.

Sir Tyrone congratulated them all at the finish and said he thought that the performance would be a success.

CHAPTER VII

Madame was drenched with sweat as she walked off the stage. Luckily, Ms. Barrington was waiting in the wings with a glass of ice water and some paper towels.

"Madame," she said, "would you like to come into my office and relax for a while?"

"Yes, darling," said Madame, and the two proceeded down the corridor.

Once into the office, Ms. Barrington showed her to a chair. "I'll turn on the air conditioning. That should cool you off."

Madame was dabbing at her forehead and the back of her neck, which were all wet. She asked Ms. Barrington if she could use the telephone. Ms. Barrington quickly brought a phone to her side.

"Thanks again, darling," said Madame. She dialed the garage where Igor was waiting. What a relief to hear his voice!

"Igor, please pick me up in ten minutes outside the opera," said Madame. He said he would bring Patrick along in case there were still newspeople outside.

"That's fine," said Madame. She began to feel better. The diva hummed a few notes. To her surprise, they fell easily into place. *I'm not hoarse at all*, she thought and began to laugh.

Ms. Barrington could not help but remark, "I'm glad that you are pleased, Madame."

Madame thought and then said, "Yes, my dear, but I hope that the critics will also take pleasure in my efforts."

"I'm sure they will," answered Ms. Barrington.

The phone rang. Ms. Barrington picked up the receiver.

"It's your chauffer, Madame. He said that he is waiting outside for you."

"Tell him I'll be right out." She got up to leave.

Ms. Barrington said, "You forgot your sweater. I'll go and get your leopard coat and beret out of your dressing room." Madame was quite disconcerted at this point and did not know exactly where she was or what her next moves were to be.

Ms. Barrington returned with the coat. "May I help you put them on?"

"Yes, darling. If you ever get tired of working for Sir Rudolph, give me a call. I'm sure you can help me. As an old lady, I shall need all the help I can get."

"You are not an old lady by any means. Right now, the whole world is your oyster. Enjoy yourself!"

Madame gave out one of her laughs and replied, "I'll try to believe that and act the part."

Madame exited Sir Rudolph's office. She did not wish to see or speak to anyone. However, she was no sooner out of the room when Professor Weigert turned the corner of the corridor. He saw her at once.

"I must tell you," he said as he walked up to her, "your rendition of 'Vissi D'Arte' was so beautiful that I could barely see the keyboard. The voice still has incomparable richness. The vocal line was of bel canto quality. I'm proud to have played the rehearsal. I shall be at the performance as will my wife Astrid."

"Thanks so much, Professor. Coming from such a fine musician as yourself, I find your words edifying. However, my car is waiting, and I must say good day to you, sir."

She finally made it to the side exit door. There were still a few reporters there, and she was glad to see Patrick waiting for her also. He quickly moved toward her and put a protective arm around her. Madame was somewhat blinded by the sunlight and the flash bulbs. She put on her sunglasses.

"Leave the lady alone!" shouted Patrick. He opened the limo door and told her to get inside. Igor pulled out the Rolls as soon as he saw in the front mirror that the two passengers were in the rear. Madame turned and thanked Patrick for helping her elude the reporters.

"I wouldn't want to be in your shoes, lady. These guys are a real pain in the . . ."

He didn't finish the line. She laughed and added that in her business, it's when they don't bother you that problems begin.

Patrick said, "You can have it. They just want to make money out of you."

She thought, *I'm beginning to think he really cares about me. I'm constantly around all these so-called intellectuals, and here a bodyguard is giving me some affection.*

The limo was going as fast as possible uptown toward the Ansonia. Patrick then asked, "Lady, could I take you out to dinner sometime?"

Madame replied, "Why not? When the proper time comes, we will do it." She handed him her professional card with her phone number on it.

He looked at her with his big blue eyes and said, "I like you very much."

She replied, "I am fond of you also."

The limo arrived at the hotel. Madame got out and told Igor and Patrick, "Thank you both. I am exhausted and must go upstairs to rest. Good day to both of you."

She swept into the Ansonia lobby again, hoping that no one would spot her. Luckily, she made it to the elevator and ascended to the floor of her apartment. She pulled at the old bell on the door, and Anita soon let her in.

"Madame, I'm so pleased that you are home."

"I don't want to talk, Anita. Just get this awful fur off me!"

Anita obliged, and Madame tossed the matching leopard-skin hat to the nearest chair.

"Draw me a hot bath, Anita, please!"

Madame walked into her beautiful boudoir and quickly took off all her clothes and finally tore off the horrible corset that had been torturing her all day. *I wish I were a beautiful goddess, like some of the blond sex symbols in the cinema. Then I wouldn't have to wear all the horrible corsets.*

Anita called from the white master bathroom to tell her that her bubble bath was ready. Madame eagerly got into the relaxing warm water and soon was humming a tune. Anita heard her and smiled.

She's having a grand time. I know she'll want her martinis when she steps out of the tub. Anita went into the kitchen and began filling the pitcher with ice, gin, and a few drops of dry vermouth. She began stirring and stirring.

Before long, Madame appeared in the kitchen doorway swathed in her green silk dressing gown and a towel wrapped around her head.

"What a sweet sound that stirring makes. I heard it while I was in the tub," said Madame. "After today's events, a drink would be just great!" she exclaimed.

"Go into the parlor, Madame. Sit in one of your magnificent chairs," said Anita. "I will bring in your drinks. I also have your favorite snacks in the oven."

"You are such a blessing," Madame said. Madame, indeed, did what Anita had advised. She sat in her favorite red brocade chair.

The events of the day filled her thoughts. *The voice still responded to my commands, but basically, I'll be glad when it's all over! Indeed, I will be more than happy to stop singing entirely once my present commitments are over.*

Anita brought in the requested martinis and snacks. She savored her first sips of the drink and began to feel relaxed. Her thoughts continued. *The older I get, the more I think that Tosca, even though it is the title role, isn't the most vital person in the opera.*

She was remembering the rendition of the "Te Deum" at the conclusion of act 1. Of course, it is the Scarpia on which the opera stands or falls.

Anita reentered the salon. "Madame, I hate to interrupt you, and I know you are tired, but the French lady is on the telephone."

Oh, she must be talking of Lily. "I'll pick the call up.

"Lily," she said as she picked up the phone, "how nice of you to call. When Anita said the French lady, I knew it was you."

"Yes, *cherie*, it is I, the person you call mon petite. I know all about *Tosca*. Stella has told me everything, as usual. I just wanted to ask, how are you doing? I hope you are not under too much stress."

"Lily darling, I'm sure that as intelligent as you are, you can fathom all the undercurrent of this situation."

"Yes, Madame," Lily went on, "I have been to Saint Jean Baptiste and said a rosary just for you."

"Thank you, my sweetness," said Madame.

"I just wanted to know if you still were going to go with me on Saturday evening to Lauritz's party as we had planned earlier."

"Of course I'm going. After all that fuss at the opera, I will deserve a little fun."

Lily went on. "I plan to attend your *Tosca* performance. Maestro Pelletier will escort me personally. Everyone is excited about this. To add to it all, many are saying that they are glad that the opera will not be *Aida*."

Madame let out a big laugh at this. "I wish I could share their joy! Lily, you are too much," said Madame.

"I'll be at your apartment at seven, and we two shall go to the Wagnerian gala together," Lily continued. "I'm going to wear something interesting, but I'm not telling you yet what it will be."

Madame answered, "I'll look forward to seeing you. Lily, you are very precious to me. I'll see you on Saturday evening."

Madame continued to sip her drink and eat the snacks. When the drink was finished, she poured herself another. She was beginning to get a bit scared of the whole situation. *Oh, you'll be great*, she tried to tell herself. But she had her doubts and wished she hadn't waited so long to present her *Tosca* to the operatic public. She thought of a review she read of Maggie Teyte, the British soprano. Teyte had waited until she was in her sixties to do Mélisande in Debussy's *Pelléas and Mélisande*. The reviews were not kind even though Maggie had been the darling of the critics.

She had only been singing in recitals in those years, mainly doing the French art song repertoire.

Mme Teyte finally consented to appear in the Debussy opera. The review read, She Waited a Long Time to Appear in the Role—Maybe Too Long!

Madame couldn't get this out of her mind. *I know the critics don't consider me their darling. I'm just an old warhorse to them.* She laid her head back and went into a sort of slumber.

There was a mental image of long ago. She was gazing into a long mirror and saw herself. She was young and beautiful. Long dark curls fell over her shoulders. The gown was low cut, showing firm breasts. The top of the costume revealed cleavage. The waist, however, was there. She was costumed in a beautiful white gown of the French Louis XVI period.

The music of *Manon Lescaut* surged through her mind. Madame had done this part many times in her young years at the Zagreb Opera. The music continued to haunt her until tears flowed down her face. In "Quelle Trine Morbide" (Behind Silken Curtains), she hummed. She had a sudden longing to be in Italy, which she loved dearly. So many memories of beauty and happiness. She began to sob openly. Anita must have heard her and came into the boudoir. Just as Madame screamed, "*Sola perduta abbondonata.*" Alone and abandoned.

Anita almost cried herself. "What on earth is wrong? Why are you calling out? Has someone said something to hurt you?"

"No, Anita," said Madame. "It is only that yearning for lost youth is often painful."

"But, Madame, you have had such a grand career!"

"Yes, I know, but years ago, everything came easy to me. Now, everything is hard work."

"You will do very well, Madame. Stop worrying," said Anita.

Anita thought, *It is all beginning to take its toll. I hope this is not too much for her.* Anita said, "Madame, I have prepared some dinner. Would you care for a little?"

"What did you prepare?" asked Madame.

"Some pasta in green basil sauce and a little baked chicken."

"That's wonderful," said Madame. "Please serve it in the kitchen. Put out two plates, we shall partake of supper together."

Madame took the towel off her head and slipped into slacks and a dark blouse. She appeared tired as she went into the kitchen.

"Well, here you are," said Anita. "Sit down and I'll bring over the food."

Madame loved pasta, and Anita gave her a generous portion along with the chicken.

"Anita, break out a bottle of Beaujolais wine," ordered Madame.

Anita sat down across the table from her mistress. She thought, *Madame rarely eats with me. She is in a strange mood.* Anita loved Madame but also was somewhat afraid of her. She always has a somewhat cold and imperious manner about her. Maybe that is why she is such a grand diva.

"Let us toast," Madame went on as she poured out two large crystal goblets of the ruby-red wine. "Here's to the arts. They are the height of achievement."

Her eyes once again glistened with moisture.

"Yes," she continued, "the arts are our heritage. Opera to me is almost sacred. When I perform now at this late stage of my career, I feel almost as if I'm participating in a sacrament."

Anita commented that she thought Madame felt this way because she is such a great artist.

Madame said that there were some who would disagree with her statement. "You know, Anita, a critic once said about me that I had a magnificent voice but that I was not an artist.

Anita did not reply. Once again, she thought any reply would be wrong to reply.

Madame then said that she was weary and wanted to go to bed. "Anita, my whole being is tired. Even as my voice is now tired and wants to go to sleep."

Anita walked with her into the bedchamber. She helped her undress and get into her nightclothes.

"Anita, please give me my sleeping mask. Awaken me at eight am sharp. I will not receive calls this night!"

Anita helped her into the huge bed. She covered her over. She put out the lights and exited the room.

CHAPTER VIII

Friday

Anita awakened early on the following morning. *She said last evening that I was to awaken her at 8:00 am.* Anita dreaded doing this once again as she knew that her mistress would not really want to rise at that hour. She began to make the coffee and, naturally, the phone rang. However, Anita decided not to answer. *I'll have my hands full, trying to get her nibs ready to go down to the Met for her wigs and costumes.*

The appointed hour soon arrived. Anita went once again to the huge door leading to her mistress's bedchamber. She slowly opened the portal and went over to pull open one of the white silken viennese shades. Madame was apparently already awake! She turned and pulled off her sleeping mask.

"Oh, darling," she said, "Anita, is it already morning?"

"Yes Madame, it is, and as you know, you are due again at the opera this morning."

"Opera, opera!" she grumbled in her low voice. "I am beginning to hate that word. Anita, come over to this bed. Help an old lady out. I feel stiff as a board."

Anita hustled over to the bed. She put out her arm as Madame grabbed it and pulled herself up. She saw her dressing gown on the chair next to her and tossed it around her.

"Anita," she went on.

"Yes, Madame?" Anita answered. Without waiting any further, she said, "Your coffee is made, and there are also rolls and strawberry jam to go with then."

"Where are they?" asked Madame.

"Out in the kitchen."

"I'll be a right out. I want to eat again in the kitchen. After all, I'm still a working girl and don't have to be served in bed."

Anita left and went into the kitchen to prepare the "La Petite Journée." Madame soon appeared. Anita served her the hot coffee and rolls.

Madame sat down and began to eat. "Stay here, Anita, please. Join me once again over a cup of coffee. You know, girl talk is always fun over coffee."

Anita was happy that Madame was in a good mood. *I'm in no mood for one of her ice-cold looks*, thought Anita.

"You know, Anita," she continued, "there are those singers who will not speak for days before a performance, especially tenors. They are the most neurotic fearful people.

"Why is that, Madame?"

Madame said because it is a different vocal category. "Those high notes are all manufactured by special vocal exercises."

"They often crack and are painful to the ear, especially high C in the tenor range. This is actually a scream, more of an animal sound. That is why Franco brings them to their feet!"

Anita said to herself, "Wow! She is really full of it this morning, isn't she?" Anita let out a big laugh she couldn't help herself.

"Do you find me so amusing?" remarked Madame. "Well my dear, that is because you do not know enough about the voice." She said imperiously.

Anita once again held her tongue.

"Well, Anita," Madame continued, "I must get ready to go back to the old house. I don't know what to wear."

Anita said, "Why don't you just put on some slacks and a nice white blouse?"

"That is a good idea. I don't care who sees me today."

Madame then went back into the room. She went directly to her makeup mirror and turned on the brightest lights. "Oh my god! What a mess! I should have seen a plastic surgeon before *Tosca*."

She began to pull her face up at the sides with her hands. A heavy coat of pancake was applied, and they're covered over with liquid makeup. She decided to wear her false eyelashes and a pale-pink lipstick. "Anita, come in quickly! Please apply the pearl nail polish to my nails."

Madame always wore pearl nail polish whether onstage or off.

Anita did as ordered. She assumed that Madame was worried about her hair. Anita then brought out a black turban and placed it over her mistress's head.

"You look fine, Madame." She helped her get into her slacks and blouse.

"Bring me my high-heeled shoes," said Madame. "I shall not have to walk much today. Call Igor and tell him I shall be downstairs in ten minutes."

Anita called Igor. She turned and saw Madame put on her mink coat and several layers of pearls. She also put her dark glasses on.

The bell rang and Anita opened the door.

Patrick stood there and said, "Igor told me that her nibs is going down to the opera again today. I came to escort her," said Patrick

Madame said, "Come over here, darling," and kissed him. "It is divine that you are here since I can't really see with these dark glasses."

She grabbed his arm and said, "Let us go quickly."

The two went to the elevator, got on, and went directly to the lobby and the waiting car. Igor was waiting. Patrick gently pushed Madame into the backseat.

She said, "Get in the rear with me. I need support today."

The familiar ride downtown went smoothly, and they soon arrived at the opera. Patrick jumped out and held the door open for her.

"You are an angel," she said to Patrick. "I don't know what I would do without you."

"Igor," she went on, "I'll see you both later. I'll call when I'm ready to leave."

Luckily, there was no one outside the Thirty-Ninth Street stage entrance when she arrived.

"Good morning," Madame said to the man at the door.

He said good morning, and she swept through the door. She took off her mink coat and threw it over her shoulders.

The workers who were milling around the halls began to greet her. In a few minutes, Sir Rudolph himself appeared. "Oh, Madame, I am so glad you are over here. I shall escort you personally to the wardrobe department."

"That won't be necessary," Madame replied. "I know perfectly well where everything is around here. Besides which, I do not want you interfering at all this morning!"

"Well," said Sir Rudolph, "aren't you in a haughty mood today?"

"No, I'm not being a bitch," she said. "I just want complete control over the events of this day."

Sir Rudolph acquiesced even though he has usually wanted to dominate every proceeding. Madame bade him good-bye and went on her way. *Where will I start*, she thought? *I think I will start with my costumes.*

She entered the room and, suddenly, Carlo and Juan, two of the dressers, were at her side. They pulled over a comfortable chair and asked her to have a seat.

"I'm so happy to see the two of you," Madame said.

"Yes," they both replied. "This whole affair is fantastic!"

Madame went on, "Do you have any ideas about what would look well on this large person in a first appearance as Floria Tosca?"

"Well, Madame, as a matter of fact," said Juan, "we have been working on a gown for the second act ever since we heard the news there would be no *Aida*."

Madame seemed happy as she had dealt with the two men before, and she trusted them. "Well, let me see the creation please!"

Carlo went into the other room and carried out a gown. He opened the garment before Madame. She looked and liked what she saw immediately!

The gown was of black velvet. The cloth, however, was not heavy in quality. There were small pearls around the top. The front center of the gown had a piece of silver material running from the bodice to the floor. The silver material was embroidered with pearls and rhinestones.

Madame stood up and her eyes were tearful as she thanked Juan and Carlo. "You two are my angels," she said almost tearfully as she hugged the two of them.

"We have worked very much on this costume," Carlo said.

Madame said, "Well, boys, now, all you have to do is get me into it."

She went behind a screen and disrobed.

"Hand me the dress." She stepped into it and held the top up in front of her. She then went out from the screen. Carlo and Juan then tried to zip up the back of the gown.

Luckily, the garment fit her!

"It looks beautiful on you," said Carlo.

Madame looked into the big mirror and was indeed pleased. "You've done very well," she said.

Juan replied, "Madame, we have been dressing you for years."

"How about my hair?"

They brought out several wigs, which she tried on.

"I don't like wigs onstage as they make me feel very hot and sweaty."

Carlo brought out a partial piece with just two curls that hung slightly over her left shoulder. He then placed a very lightweight diamond tiara on her head.

Madame liked what she saw and said, "That's it, what do you two think?"

Both men said that she looked stunning.

She went on. "Tomorrow is the big day. I'll be happy when *La Tosca* is history. Do you think the critics will be kind?"

Juan answered, "What do you care? You have sung here hundreds of times."

Carlos said, "We all have confidence in you. I'm sure you'll be great."

Madame said, "Well then, fellows, I'll see you tomorrow. I'll be here once again at eleven am to walk through the set of act 2. Please bring the gown and wiglet to my dressing room in the morning."

The two men said yes to her request. Madame exited the room and went to look for the phone.

Ms. Barrington appeared just around the next turn. "Oh," said Ms. Barrington. "I'm so glad that I encountered you. I was going to call you because Sir Rudolph wanted me to remind you that the act 2 sets of *Tosca* will be in place on stage at ten am tomorrow."

"Thank you," said Madame. "Since there is to be no dress rehearsal, I shall want to walk around the set to get some idea of what and where everything will be."

Ms. Barrington went on to say that there have been a tremendous amount of calls to Sir Rudolph. "I think they all want to come to hear you as Tosca."

Madame did not comment but simply asked if one could use the telephone.

"Of course," replied Ms. Barrington. "Come into the office and take your time."

Madame called Igor and asked him to pick her up at the stage entrance. The diva was very tired of everything and everybody at this juncture. *If only I would get on a ship and sail far away from all this. I don't care where the ship would take me.* Igor soon arrived and got her into the limo.

"Let's go for a drive somewhere," she said. "I would like to get away from New York City for a few hours."

Igor said, "How about going up to Connecticut."

"That would be wonderful. Just drive, and I will tell you when to stop. Take the shore road. I'd like to look at the sea." The duo headed north and into the Bronx.

What an awful place, thought Madame. *Such squalor!* America certainly is a land of contrasts, great wealth, and then into complete poverty. They went farther. The towers of Co-op City appeared. The complex looked like a prison to her. Finally, she began to see some trees and individual homes. *I guess we're finally passing middle class America.* There were carefully kept lawns and a few above-ground swimming pools. It was all quite depressing to her. *I have lived in a fantasy world all my life. The artificiality of the opera world is awful, but this is worse! At least I know that the people in the operatic world are mostly phony hypocrites. What is worse in this country, being poor or having to commute for hours on a stuffy train to get to work?* Worst of all, they have to pay most of what they earn into taxes, pension programs, or medical plans.

The ride was good for her. She was forgetting about *Tosca*. Thank God! "Igor, keep driving. Go as fast as you are allowed. I'm getting a kick out of this ride. What do Americans mean by that silly expression *kick?*"

She liked Ethel Merman and began humming "I Get a Kick Out of You." Merman sings like a dramatic tenor. The registration is the same.

The scenery began to get prettier, as the sign read You Are Now Entering The Great State of Connecticut. On they drove. She looked at the signs—Stamford, Bridgeport, New London. They all looked the same. Broken down old factories and shabby housing projects. *I thought this was the richest state? The rich must be somewhere else!*

Finally, she began to see some green. There were miles of lowlands. The sea was mixed with the flowing greenery. There were some scattered houses appearing in this sea of grass. They looked like sunken cathedrals. She spotted a sign that read "To the Beach."

"Igor, follow that sign!"

He did as she bade, and soon they were at an open beach.

"Stop here," she ordered. *I'll need my mink coat here.* She threw it over her shoulders.

"Madame," said Igor, "please put a scarf over your head. You do not wish to catch a cold before tomorrow!"

She took off her shoes. They were like torture chambers with high heels. She began to walk barefoot to the sea. This area reminded her of the marches on the East Coast of Italy. She took in a few breaths of air. *Ah,* she thought, *such freedom! I can't wait until I retire. I'm so sick of the pretense and charade of the opera. Every time some new singer makes a record, the critics all go mad! Even the radio never stops praising the new Farrar or Caruso. I think it's a cover-up. They all are paid by the recording companies to praise them. The laugh of it all is, once they sing in the big house, they are barely heard over the orchestra. The orchestra is carefully held down by the maestro, who has found a new pet.*

She took in a few more breaths of sea air. *I guess Igor is right. I had better return home before I catch a bit of a cold.* She trod back to Igor and returned to her plush backseat.

"Did you enjoy your walk, Madame?" he asked.

"Yes, my dear. Real air is nice after all the hot air of the opera."

They both laughed

"What now?" he asked.

"Oh, just go back to the highway, and we shall return to the city."

She turned her head toward the rear window for more glimpses of the scenery. The sun was just going down in a big red ball and seemed to be falling into the sea, which was glittering under its incandescence. The clouds also appeared to be turning pink. *Ah, if I could only paint like Turner or Monet,* she thought.

The drive back to the city was long and dreary. Most of the traffic was going north. The poor commuters were making their journey home from work.

They finally arrived back to the Ansonia. Igor walked her to the door.

"Pick me up right here tomorrow at ten am," she said.

"Yes, Madame," he replied.

She rang the bell and Anita soon appeared at the door.

"Madame, I thought that you would never return home." She went on to say that the phone rang and rang but that she did not answer.

"Good," said Madame. "The inexorable only awaits, and no phone call can change that. I do not wish to speak with anyone. Let us continue with this gossip blackout.

Anita laughed. "Are you hungry, Madame?"

"Yes, I am very hungry. Make me a filet mignon with some spinach and potatoes."

Anita said, "Fine, and while I'm doing this, shall I prepare a dry martini?"

Madame nodded an emphatic yes! She went into her boudoir, changed her clothes, and put on her green dressing gown. Anita had turned on a tape of Bach.

Madame walked back into the huge parlor and sat in her favorite red chair. Anita soon bought the Martini, and Madame was relaxing listening to the Bach.

It was a concerto for harpsichord and chamber orchestra. *Bach is the greatest of all composers*, thought Madame. *I never tire of him.*

She desperately wanted to get her mind away from opera! Anita helped her get ready for bed. She crawled into her nest and was soon asleep.

CHAPTER IX

Saturday

Anita awakened early and winded her way quietly into Madame's boudoir. As usual, she pulled up the viennese Curtains very lightly, and as usual, Madame awakened. Her first words were "Are you packing for the trip to Europe?"

"Europe?" said Anita. "No, Madame, today is your big *Tosca* day."

"It is too early for creating a farce. Reality is bad enough," said Madame.

Anita had already left the room to get Madame's breakfast. It soon arrived. Anita set it down on the table near Madame's red chair.

"On a silver platter no less," said Mme. "I'm not doing *Salome* today, am I? I really don't feel like dancing or singing for that matter. Maybe I should cancel. Sir Rudolph would really go mad if I did. Anita, what do you think?"

Anita again gave no answer.

Madame began to sip her coffee. "Oh, I guess I'll have to go through with the horror show. I created my own monster."

"We all do, Madame. That is life," replied Anita.

"You are correct again, Anita." She began to get dressed. "I'll just wear slacks and a blouse. Anita, what time is it?"

"Nine o'clock," replied Anita.

Oh my god, thought Madame! *Igor will be here at ten am to pick me up.* She quickly pulled herself together. The diva got up and walked into the living room. She gave a quick glance into the mirror. *How awful I look*, she thought. Quickly she walked over to the piano. *The voice, I almost forgot. Do I have a voice today?* She played a few scales and hummed along with them. *At least, I'm not hoarse. Nor do I have a cold. Thank God!*

"Anita," she called once again, "get me a turban."

Anita brought one in, and Madame placed it on her head. She applied a light pink lipstick. "That will be it. The boys will make me up down at the house. Oh, my nails, Anita. Bring my pearl nail polish."

Madame always wore this polish onstage whether in fashion or not. She sat down on the couch and waited for Anita. "Anita, darling, please paint my nails."

Anita did the best she could as Madame seemed quite nervous. Anita again reassured the diva that she would give a grand performance. Madame waited for her nail polish to dry.

"Anita, be a darling and get me some dark glasses? The darker the better, and please get me my mink coat."

Anita complied, and Madame put on the dark glasses and her mink coat. The phone rang. It was Igor.

"I'm downstairs with the limo. Is she ready?" he asked Anita.

"As ready as she ever will be," Anita replied.

Igor said that he would send Patrick up to escort her down. Anita repeated the message.

"Oh, I'm so happy that Patrick will help me. I want to get out of here and into the limo."

The bell rang, and there stood a smiling blue-eyed Patrick. Madame seemed happy to see him. He grabbed her arm to support her.

"Handsome is as handsome does," she said.

"How are you, honey," he said.

"Honey, no one has called me that in years." If ever, she let out a laugh.

"You are a honey," he repeated. "Let's get going."

He closed the door behind them and took her down the elevator to the waiting car. He got her into the backseat, and they headed down to Thirty-Ninth Street. Madame was feeling scared to death. All sorts of terrible things were going through her mind. *Suppose the fans resent me for replacing an idol? What if I crack on a high C? I'm too old for this!*

This type of gibberish went through her brain. Patrick tried to reassure her by putting his arm up around her on the top of the rear seat of the car.

"I know you don't want to speak, honey," he said. "I'll understand."

Madame wanted to open the door and jump out. She really didn't want to go through with this. However, she restrained herself. Finally, the limo reached Thirty-Ninth Street. Igor stopped the car. Patrick opened the door, got up, and offered her a strong hand. She grabbed it, and he pulled her out of the car.

"Leave me now," she said. The great diva pulled back her shoulders and proudly strode into the door of the house. She was, however, relieved that no one was there except the doorman. He opened the stage door for her.

"Everybody around here is on your side today," he said with a smile.

"Thanks, darling," she replied. Suddenly, Ms. Barrington appeared.

She said, "Sir Rudolph asked me to be here today in order to offer you assistance if needed."

Madame was pleased. "If you could bring me a cup of tea."

"Yes, I would enjoy that."

Madame went directly to her dressing room. Her gown was there just as Carlos and Juan had promised. *They are so good*, she thought. *The pay they receive is not that much. However, they must think highly of me to have done all these gracious things.*

There was a knock on the door. It was Ms. Barrington. "Here's your tea, Madame."

"Thank you so much, darling."

"Are you feeling well today, Madame?"

"Yes, I'm getting over being nervous. I'll do as well as I can do and that's it," continued Madame.

"Well," added Ms. Barrington. "Is there anything else I can do?"

"Yes, walk with me to the stage."

Ms. Barrington said gladly. "You know, Madame, the stage bands were ordered by Sir Rudolph to have the act 2 set on stage for you. Let's go see what it looks like." Madame was glad not to be alone. The two women walked toward the stage. When they arrived backstage, Madame said to Ms. Barrington that she could leave her now.

She walked onto the stage from the left side. The vast auditorium was empty. Madame looked out at the thousands of empty red velvet seats. *Soon they will be filled.*

I can't believe that they will tear this old house down. She then began to walk around the set. *Opera*, she thought, *is a sort of sacrament. There is Scarpia's desk. I must find the wine decanter, the glasses, and of course, the cutlery.* There was a table with these objects nearby. She walked over, and her hand gently felt for the knife. She picked it up. Her hand trembled slightly. *I guess I am nervous,* she thought. *Good, that is the way I will be. My hand will also tremble in the performance.*

She was looking at the knife when Sir Tyrone entered. He said, "You will be wonderful. Don't have a care. I have spoken to Sherrill, and he seems assured of his role."

"Well," she added, "I don't want him to throw me around too much. Do you think I should kneel during the "Vissi D'Arte"?

Sir Tyrone said "If you can" but was afraid to ask if she could get up again afterward.

"Maybe the young Sherrill will give me his hand." She seemed to read his lips.

"I'll tell him to do so," said Sir Tyrone.

"Shall I tell Mario anything?" asked Sir Tyrone?

"No, he and I have been onstage together many times in *Chenier* and *Aida*. We are like siblings. There will be no problems," said Madame.

"I'll be in the wings during the performance," he said in a reassuring manner.

He walked off, and Madame trod over the entire stage. She knew the best places from which to project the voice. *Thomas will be conducting. He is such a kind person. I don't care how loud the orchestra is in act 2. In fact, the louder the better. However, I want the orchestra to be soft in "Vassi D'Arte." I will sing all pianissimo in that aria, and then they will have to play carefully. That's enough of this. I must get back to my dressing room.*

She arrived there, and Juan and Carlos were already waiting for her. "Where do we start, Madame?" asked Carlos.

"I must get out of my clothes." She went behind the screen and came out in her underclothes. "How's that for an old lady?"

Juan laughed and said, "Well, Madame, just a few pounds here and there."

They had brought a trunk of apparel with them. He pulled out a corset.

"Come over here. Put that around me and pull the strings in the back tightly." Carlos did the best he could. "But, Madame," he said, "you don't want the corset to be too tight."

"Don't' worry, darling. I was breathing before you were born."

They both laughed again. They slipped the black gown over her head. Thank God she got into it!

"Look, guys, I'm in this now. So what are we going to do for act 1 and act 3?"

Juan pulled a gray silk cape out of the trunk. The cape also had sleeves. They helped Madame put it on.

"Perfect." she said. So now all was ready for the performance.

"Come with me to my dressing room," she said. They did as she said. Once in the room, she went over to the makeup table and sat down.

She turned on the bright lights around the mirror. Juan and Carlos began to apply her makeup.

"Not too dark, boys. Remember, this is supposed to be Rome and not the Nile." They all giggled and continued to make her up.

"That's fine," said Madame. She walked over to the big wall mirror and applied her own lipstick. All too soon, she heard a voice call.

"Ten minutes to curtain time!"

She walked slowly to the side entrance of the stage. Sir Rudolph went out in front of the gold curtains to announce that Mme Rinaldi would not sing. The opera had been changed, and *Tosca* would be given. The title role would be sung by Mme Godanov. There was not much reaction by the audience. They probably all knew the whole story by now since the entire matter had already appeared in the newspapers.

She heard the applause as Thomas appeared on the podium. Soon she could hear Mario's huge voice singing his first aria. Someone seemed to gently nudge her onstage, and she was singing "Mario, Mario."

Act 1 went well and ended with a bombastic "Te Deum." The rest of the opera seemed to go by as if she were in a dream. There was a big ovation after the "Vissi D'Atre."

Finally, at the end, she took her solo bow, and flowers and confetti were thrown onstage from the upper tiers.

Sir Rudolph was backstage as she walked off. He said, "I knew you would do well," as if taking personal credit for the success. She found her way back to the dressing room. Luckily, Anita was waiting for her. Anita threw her arm around Madame and gave her a big kiss.

"I'm so proud of you," Anita said. "It was a grand performance."

"Thanks, darling, but I'm all wet with sweat. Get me out of these costumes."

"But, Madame, there is a line of well-wishers outside in the corridor."

The porters were already bringing in baskets and bouquets of flowers.

"Is Patrick out there? If he is, get him in here," ordered Madame.

Anita quickly went out and shut the door behind her. Madame bolted it. Patrick was soon pounding on the door. Madame called, "I'll let you and Anita in here but no one else." Patrick was trying to hold the adoring fans including the press at bay. Madame opened the door, and in came her blue-eyed Irishman with Anita in tow. Once again they closed the door behind them.

"There are some big wheels out there, including the governor and Cardinal Spellman," said Patrick.

Madame thought, *I must get to confession, but not at this moment. Also, I'm not running for political office either!* "Patrick, please go out and tell them that Madame is completely exhausted by her art and cannot see anyone now. She will get back to everyone on another occasion."

Somehow or another, she reached the Thirty-Ninth Street exit. By some miracle, Patrick was there. He hustled her into the waiting limo. Igor was happy when he heard the back door of the vehicle slam shot.

"Get back to Ansonia as quickly as possible," Madame ordered. Patrick was next to her in the rear seat.

"You really knocked them for a loop," he said. "I never heard such yelling. It was like Di Maggio at Yankee Stadium."

Madame was in a trance and did not say a word. They finally arrived at the Ansonia. She pulled at the old doorbell, and Anita let her in.

"Madame, I have your martinis ready," she said.

"Get me out of these awful clothes and I'll drink them."

So the event had finally transpired and ended.

CHAPTER X

The Saturday Night Party

Madame had bathed and was again in her green dressing gown. She wearily asked Anita what she should wear.

"I already have the dress ready."

"Bring it to me," ordered Madame.

The garment was a three-quarter-length silk dress, also of mint green and also bought in Italy. Anita lovingly helped her mistress get into it. She combed her hair back. Anita then said, "I brought the tiara back from the opera, Tosca."

She placed it on Madame's head and also draped the real La Scala pearls around her neck. Anita once again made her up and applied a luminous pink lipstick.

"Spray me with Chanel please?" said Madame.

Anita was so proud of her. "I must say that you proved again today that you are indeed a very great artist."

Madame still was smarting from the critics and said, "They will never agree with you."

The bell rang and Anita walked down the long hall and opened the door. There stood Lily. She was in a pink satin gown with a hoop skirt. Her dark hair was all in long curls, and she wore a black velvet band around her neck. Her feet were adorned with pink slippers, which had stiletto heels.

"Tell Madame I'm here," said Lily.

Anita did as she bade and guided her gently into Madame's huge music room. The two women hugged each other, and Lily gave Madame a gentle kiss on the cheek.

Lily said, "Words could not describe your achievement this afternoon as *Tosca*, Madame."

Madame replied, "Thank you, darling, but I'm happy that it is all over."

Madame went on to tell Lily that she looked lovely and just like a belle from the Old South.

"Yes," said Lily, "I just got off the riverboat."

Madame laughed and said, "This is not a showboat."

Lily retorted, "Let's make believe."

Madame asked Anita to bring her a black lace shawl that she had bought in Capri. Anita brought it to her, and she tossed it over her shoulder. "Well, Lily," she asked, "are we ready?"

Lily took her by the arm, and the two were on their way. They were like two young girls giggling their way out of the apartment.

They took the elevator up to the tenth floor. The door opened and they couldn't believe their eyes. The huge hallway, which extended forever, was filled with tables. Each table was covered with a white tablecloth and adorned by settings of exquisite silverware and crystal glasses. Flowers were all over the place. The two women were wide-eyed with delight.

There were waiters dressed in tuxedos with white shirts, red cummerbunds, and red bow ties. The headwaiter suddenly appeared and asked if he could escort them into the huge apartment. He said his name was Bernard.

"Well, Bernie," said Madame, "I am Rosina and this is Ms. Scarlet."

Lily opened a big fan of feathers and began to fan the two of them. Madame grabbed one of Bernie's arms and Lily the other.

"Escort us into the chamber," ordered Madame.

They were both still giggling. Bernie brought them to a huge gray-haired man. He, of course, recognized them. The Great Dane greeted them each with a smooch on the cheek. Next to him was a diminutive woman. "This is Kleinchen," which is how he referred to his wife. She was, of course, very charming.

Lauritz said, "I would like for you to meet two of my friends." They were two huge women. "This is Kirsten, and this is Helen."

Madame admired both of them.

Lauritz said, "I have the good fortune to sing with two great Isoldes. Kirsten has a voice like a shining diamond, and Helen's voice is like a beautiful ruby."

Lily said, "How can you choose between such precious jewels?"

They all laughed. Lily excused herself as also did Madame.

She said to Madame, "Let's circulate."

There were many famous people in the crowd. Among them were people from the Hollywood group. Lauritz was making movies, and Lily had appeared in a few herself. Madame noticed a beautiful woman with red hair.

"Isn't that Myrna Loy?" she asked.

"Yes!" said Lily.

"She really is a beauty."

They began to move toward her. However, they were interrupted by a man's voice. "Hello, Ms. Nightingale. How about giving out with the belle song? No one can sing it like you, Lily," he went on.

"This is Mme Godanov," Lily said.

"Baby, I know your voice from records. It is the greatest! How come I never signed you up for MGM?"

Madame smiled but made no reply. He suddenly gulped down what seemed to be a whiskey sour and walked away.

They then continued to move toward the red-haired woman. She saw them and came over. "Why, Lily! How are you?"

"I'm fine, Myrna," said Lily.

Madame introduced herself.

Myrna said, "Your voice is magnificent. Wow! If I could only sing like you!"

Madame replied, "I love your movies, especially the Thin Man series. Everybody I know sees them."

Lily reiterated her praises.

"Thanks, ladies, but that guy you were just talking to fired me years ago."

"Why?" asked Lily.

"He called me into the office at MGM."

"I hear you are angry at me," said Louey.

"I sure am," said the film star.

"Why are you continuing to show my films in Germany and Austria?"

"I show films wherever I want. You just appear in them," said Louey. "However, I own them. If you don't like what I do, you can retire. You have seen your best years anyway." He took out her contract and tore it up!

Madame smirked and said, "That sounds like another executive I know."

"Oh well, let's not spoil our party," said Myrna.

Myrna then moved on, and Lily and Madame continued to meet more friends and colleagues. Dinner was served, and the evening came to a grand conclusion. Madame bade good night to Lily and returned to her apartment. She took the elevator down and went in exhausted. Anita opened the door.

Madame said, "Help me to bed. I'm completely done in. It has been quite a day!"

CHAPTER XI

The big challenge of *Tosca* had been met! Madame really felt now that her singing career was ended. Many offers came from various opera houses; however, Madame did not accept them.

My voice is tired and wants to go to sleep, she thought.

She did, however, want to sing at the closing gala of the old opera house. This was quite a night. She remembered waiting backstage to hear Lily sing "Caro Nome." Ah! That was a lovely rendition of the aria.

Madame then went on to sing the final duet from *Andrea Chénier* with Richard.

She laughed before they went onstage since she heard someone say, "Here come the big mouths now!" Madame had insisted the duet be sung in the original key and not a half tone lower as is sometimes done.

She sang as loudly as she could.

These two great singers received a thunderous and unending ovation. The old house was soon closed, and her career was finished. Madame rode home in her car with Patrick by her side. *I'm going on to a new and beautiful life.*

That was her destiny.